Sinful Behavior

Michael "OoDoo" Smith

Michael "Oodoo" Smith

This book is a work of fiction, names, characters, places and events are a product of the authors imagination or used fictitiously. Any resemblance to actual events locales or person living or dead is a coincidence.

Author Michael "OoDoo" Smith

Edited Teairo Preston

Cover Design Kimberly Wooo-Smith

Sinful Behavior

Copyright © 2020 Michael "OoDoo" Smith

All rights reserved.

ISBN - 978-1-7358661-0-9

Michael "Oodoo" Smith

Dedication

This book is dedicated to my sisters Teairo and Tiuna Preston…Thanks for being the loving sisters to me and the best aunts my kids could want…. I love yall wit ya ugly asses!! LOL!!!

Sinful Behavior

Word From The Wise

As long as they are eating off your plate, they will never get full!

Michael "Oodoo" Smith

Contents

Chapter 1..7

Chapter 2..29

Chapter 3..46

Chapter 4..63

Chapter 5..94

Chapter 6..129

Chapter 7..158

Chapter 8..178

Chapter 9..203

Chapter 10..222

Chapter 11..247

Sinful Behavior

Acknowledgements

I give all praise and thanks to my LORD and SAVIOR JESUS CHRIST !! Without you my LORD I am nothing!!! Sending all my love to the worlds top designer, my wife Kim Wooo! I LOVE you ugly !!! To my kids and family yall already know what it is, NOTHING BUT LOVE !!! Thanks to anyone who has supported my works of literature!! I truly appreciate YOU ! GOD BLESS!!!

Michael "Oodoo" Smith

CHAPTER 1

"There is nothing or nobody who can move mountains for you, but our Jesus Christ can do anything for you as long as you have faith and believe." Pastor Elijah Woods smiled as he listened to his congregation go wild from the words he preached. He wiped the sweat from his face with his Versace handkerchief, then he looked at the members of the church as some of them screamed hallelujah and amen. A few members even fell out claiming to have the Holy Ghost. Look at Sista Mathews' sexy ass. I told her about falling out on the floor, busting her legs open, knowing she aint got on any panties. Ain trippin tho. Let her do her thang because she makes sure

Sinful Behavior

that her husband deposits two grand a week into my offering plates, thought Elijah as he thought about the fact that he made ten times the money at his new church than he made at the old church. He collected offerings for Sunday School, Tithes and Offering, Love Offering, Building Funds, Pastor Anniversary and anything else he decided to pass the offering plate around for on any given Sunday.

"The doors of the church are open!" Elijah signaled to the deacons for them to sit out the chairs for anyone who wanted to be saved, repent or claim New Life Ministry as their new church home. The choir sang "Jesus is on the main line" while the congregation waited to see if anyone new was gonna join the church. Seeing that nobody was interested in joining his church, Elijah decided to end the service.

"Since nobody wants to be saved or join our church family today, service is over. I hope to see you all at Bible study on Wednesday." With that said, Elijah walked out of the pulpit and started strolling to the entrance of the sanctuary to shake some hands, give some hugs and receive flirts from the women who had attended service.

One Bruno Magli sharkskin loafer at a time, Elijah glided down the aisles filling the air with his expensive

"Straight to Heaven" men's fragrance as it jumped off of his all white Hermes suite. All white was Elijah's trademark. Some of the younger members of the church called Elijah "Reverend Cocaine." When Elijah asked them why they called him that, they told him it was because he be cleaner than a brick of fish scale cocaine. Elijah asked them to please not call him "Reverend Cocaine," but they still insisted.

"Pastor Woods, that was an amazing sermon you preached today." Sista Fallon Davis said as she opened her arms to hug Elijah. She didn't care one bit that her husband was standing behind her as she intimately embraced Elijah, placing her 46 double D breasts against his chest.

"Thank you, Sista Davis. And Brother Davis! How are you doing today?" Elijah said as he practically pried Sista Davis off of him.

"I'm good, Pastor. I can't wait to see you on the court this comin' up weekend." Brotha Davis said, smiling. He really thinks his team is going to beat us, thought Elijah, referring to the church league basketball tournament, which will be played in the full-size gymnasium that is connected to the rear of the church. The basketball league is

Sinful Behavior

sponsored by Global Mercedes Benz Dealership where Deacon Jones works and where Elijah bought his last two vehicles.

"Can't wait to see you on the court either, Brotha Davis." You need to be more concerned about your wife rather than a damn basketball game 'cause she been sucking Deacon Jones's dick every chance she gets, thought Elijah as he shook Brotha Davis's hand.

"Got damn! Lord, please forgive me!" Elijah said to himself when his eyes were filled with the beautiful Miss Tasha Caine. Kalawwd have mercy, thought Elijah. The tight fitting, sleeveless sunflower yellow Chanel dress Tasha had on was basically painted onto her five-foot six-inch, 145-pound frame, which was coated with caramel brown skin that looked as sweet as a pack of Sugar Babies candy.

"Hemm hemm! How are you doing, Sista Caine?" Elijah had to clear his throat before speaking. This muthafucka is so damn fine, thought Elijah as he fought the temptation to grope himself.

"I'm good, Pastor! I just came to tell you that mama cooked if you wanna stop by and get you a plate." Said Tasha. I want to eat you right now, thought Elijah, feeling like he was being lured by Tasha's chinky, hazel brown eyes. He wanted so bad to run his fingers through her thousand-dollar Brazilian sew-in weave, which looked like it was her real hair. Elijah started imagining he was sucking on Tasha's plump lips that looked like Jolly Ranchers from the lipstick she was wearing.

"Tell Mother Caine that I will be there no later than three o'clock, so put me a plate up!" Elijah flashed his invisible sets and gently squeezed Tasha's arm. When he let go of her, she reached up and picked a piece of lent out of his wavy, temp fade with her soft, manicured fingers.

"Okay. I'll be waiting!" Tasha turned to walk away but caught sight of Elijah and Deacon Jones gawking at her juicy booty, and she turned back around to face them.

"One other thing. Deacon Jones, could you please stay out of my inbox and DM. I've told you several times that I don't want anything to do with you!" Tasha turned around and walked away leaving Deacon Jones looking stupid. Elijah looked at Deacon Jones in disbelief, shaking his head.

"What? Come on bruh! Look at all that! Can you blame me for trying to get some of that?" Deacon Jones pleaded his case.

Sinful Behavior

"Bruh, you know the rules. Let them come to you!" Elijah mumbled so that only Deacon Jones could hear him.

"You right bruh. My bad!" Deacon Jones nodded his head as he apologized.

Elijah shook hands, gave advice and kissed enough old women for a lifetime. Then he went to his office while Deacon Jones went to the secretary's office to join the other Deacons to help them count up the money that was collected in service.

"Wheww shit!" Elijah sighed in relief as he sat down in his Victorian leather recliner. He reached into the small fridge that sat next to his desk and pulled out a bottle of Patron and some pineapple juice. He fixed himself a mixed drink.

"Ahhh! I needed that!" Elijah said after he turned up his drink.

Elijah Malikah Woods was born in Atlanta, Georgia at the Grady Hospital to the young Reverend James Woods and Brenda Woods. Elijah made the married couples fourth child in a row. James Jr., their oldest child, was four when Elijah was born. Then there was Felicia who was three and Renee who was two at the time of Elijah's birth.

Michael "Oodoo" Smith

Reverend James Woods worked fulltime for a railroad company and he was the pastor at Woods Memorial Baptist, which was the church he grew up in on the Southside of Atlanta. When Elijah was ten, his father James died from cancer at the young age of 36, leaving his wife Brenda to raise four kids on her own with only twenty-thousand dollars from an insurance policy and no work experience. Brenda tried her best to keep the kids in line, but her best wasn't enough to stop James Jr. from selling crack just a few months after his daddy had passed away. Knowing that the money from her husband's life insurance policy wasn't gonna last long, Brenda figured that she would get a job since the kids were old enough to stay at home by themselves. Things worked out well for Brenda for a few months while she worked second shift at a local diner, but with a teenage son in the streets dabblin' with drugs and two daughters in middle school, it wasn't long before Brenda lost total control of her household.

As the years passed, James Jr. taught Elijah everything that he learned in the streets about everything from guns, to women and drugs. James Jr. made Elijah promise him that he would never use or sell drugs. Elijah promised James Jr. that he would never get involved with drugs in any type of way. Elijah became a major fan of rap

Sinful Behavior

music and street lingo. Growing up, he realized that he was a people's person, and everyone seemed to like him. When he was in the ninth grade, he found James Jr.'s weed stash. Since everyone was at the hospital with Renee while she gave birth to her baby boy, Elijah decided to roll up a blunt. He tried to roll the blunt for over an hour before he finally got it rolled to the point where it was smokable. Elijah was on cloud nine and halfway done with smoking the blunt when James Jr. walked in the house and caught him smoking, trying to blow O's of smoke with his mouth. James Jr. beat up Elijah bad, blackening both his eyes. When Brenda came home and saw Elijah's face, she started cussin' James Jr. out until he explained to her why he beat up Elijah. Brenda apologized to James Jr. then she told Elijah he deserved what he got. The next morning Brenda made Elijah go to school with black eyes and all.

Elijah was embarrassed as hell as he walked down the hallways of Bannaker High school. He had never felt so belittled in all of his life. All the kids were pointing fingers and talking about him. A few of his teachers even pulled him out of class and asked him what happened to him. That day Elijah sat by himself at lunch. He was so mortified that he couldn't eat. He chewed on one fry for five minutes with his head down, while he replayed the scene of James jr. beating him up in his mind. Someone sat a tray on the table then sat down across from Elijah snapping him out of his daydream causing him to look up.

"My father says that prayer is healing. Give me your hands so that we can pray!" Cynthia Dawson was one of the prettiest girls in the school. She was a beautiful brown skinned girl with a nice shape and long pretty hair that ran past her shoulders. She and Elijah had indulged in a few minor conversations, but never anything serious.

"It's funny that you say that because my pops told me the same thing when I fell off my bike when I was five years old." Elijah handed Cynthia his hands and they bowed their heads.

"Dear Lord, please heal my friend Elijah and make his road smooth from any bumps in his life. Amen!" Cynthia's prayer seemed to instantly make Elijah feel better. When they opened their eyes, the entire lunchroom was looking at them.

From that day forward, Elijah and Cynthia ate lunch together. They eventually started growing feelings for one another. Six weeks after their prayer, Elijah asked Cynthia to be his girlfriend, but she wasn't the person who could give him his answer. Elijah would have to ask her father.

Sinful Behavior

The only problem was that Cynthia wasn't gonna be able to introduce Elijah to her father because her father had told her that if a man wants to be with her, then he must be man enough to find her father to introduce himself and ask on his own like a man is supposed to do.

"How will I find your daddy?" Elijah asked Cynthia as they ate their lunch.

"Simple, he's the pastor at a New Life Ministry Church. Come to church Sunday." Cynthia stood up from the table then she leaned down and kissed Elijah on his cheek.

"I hope to see you at church Sunday!" Cynthia left Elijah sitting at the table dizzy from the effects of her kiss.

Sunday..........

"Shawty, I'll be out here at one o'clock to pick you up, Shawty. Put this in the pimp's collection plate and tell God I said what's up." James Jr. gave Elijah twenty dollars.

"Okay Shawty, I'll be out here on time." Elijah got out of James Jr.'s car and walked up to the church dressed in a button-down Polo shirt, a pair of khakis and some penny loafers. He could hear the choir singing as he approached the entrance to the church.

"Amazing Grace

How sweet the sound

Cynthia sang along with the rest of the choir as she watched Elijah come through the door of the sanctuary. She couldn't prevent from smiling when she saw him. Elijah walked closer to the front of the sanctuary and took a seat in the fourth row. He looked up at the choir and saw Cynthia, which caused him to smile. As Elijah sat during the service, he figured that the man sitting behind the podium in the pulpit wearing a baby blue three-piece suit with the blue gators to match, must be Cynthia's father.

Elijah kept his eyes on Pastor Dawson who sat behind the podium occasionally sipping orange juice from a glass while he tapped his foot on the floor to the sound of the choir. Later in the service Pastor Dawson stood from his seat and began preaching. The entire church acted as if God himself was in the pulpit. Elijah sat in amazement as Pastor Dawson preached and the people in the crowd started catching the Holy Ghost. People started running and shouting all around Elijah. Elijah looked to the pulpit and all of a sudden, his father appeared in the pulpit,

Sinful Behavior

floating in the air wearing all white with a halo of gold around his head. Elijah thought he was hallucinating. He closed his eyes and when he re-opened them, his father was still there glowing, looking angelic.

"My son, this can be you. You have what it takes to be a great pastor and have a big congregation behind you." James told Elijah then he disappeared from his son's vision. Elijah looked around the church to see if anyone else had seen what he had just saw. Dad is right! I can be a great pastor, thought Elijah.

"The doors of the church are open! Is there anyone here who is lost and needs to be found? If so, we have a home for you right here in the house of the Lord." Pastor Dawson said into the mic as the deacons sat out the chairs for anyone who wanted to be saved, repent or become a member of the church. Elijah got up from his seat and walked up to the chairs and took a seat.

"Hallelujah! Amen. Praise God!" Pastor Dawson screamed into the mic and the church went wild as he walked out of the pulpit to Elijah.

"How are you doing son?" Pastor Dawson asked Elijah.

"I'm fine sir!" Elijah replied.

"Give me your name and tell me what assistance we can be of yours today at A New Life Ministry."

Elijah said, "I wanna become a member of your church and one day I wanna become the pastor." Elijah spoke with confidence.

"Hallelujah! Praise God! Hallelujah! Y'all heard the young man! Line up so we can welcome him to his new church home at A New Life Ministry!" Pastor Dawson ordered the congregation.

The members of the church lined up and one by one they walked to the front. They shook Pastor Dawson's hand first. Next, they shook Deacon Jones' hand and last they shook Elijah's hand. When Cynthia made it to Elijah, she hugged him instead of shaking his hand. Pastor Dawson was taken by surprise of his daughter's actions, but his wife Pam, who was behind Cynthia in line wasn't surprised because her daughter had already told her about Elijah. When everyone shook Elijah's hand, church service was over, and Pastor Dawson invited Elijah to his office. So, Elijah followed behind him. Pastor Dawson opened his office door and Elijah got the shock of his life when he saw a naked woman standing in the pastor's office.

Sinful Behavior

"Sista Malone, what the hell are you doing in my office?" Pastor Dawson quickly pulled Elijah into the office and shut the door before someone else walked by and saw the scene. Elijah couldn't help but to notice how big Sista Malone's nipples were.

"You know got damn well why I'm here naked. It's the second Sunday of the month and I want that dick! I don't care nothin' about that lil nigga being in here. I want my issue!" Sista Malone meant she didn't give a damn about Elijah being there because she cocked her leg up on the pastor's desk and patted her pussy. Her pussy was so hairy that Elijah couldn't make out what it was. Pastor Dawson walked up to Sista Malone.

"Please baby, don't do this right now. Put your clothes on. I'll be over to your house no later than four o'clock to bless you down. Give me a few hours to get things squared away at home and I'll be straight over there. Ya hear me?" Pastor Dawson ran his fingers through Sista Malone's hair and then kissed her on the cheek. She melted like ice cubes on a hot summer day from Pastor Dawson's smooth touch and tranquilizing voice. Sista Malone smiled as big as the sun.

Michael "Oodoo" Smith

"Okay Big Daddy. I'll be waiting for you!" Sista Malone took her leg from off the desk and picked up her clothes from off the couch. She quickly threw on her dress, heels and hat then left out of Pastor Dawson's office. Pastor Dawson looked at Elijah

"Are you sure you still wanna become a pastor now that you see that your office might be filled with uninvited naked women who are demanding sex from you?" He asked Elijah as he sat down behind his desk and pulled out a bottle of Crown Royal.

"Sir, I'm sure about becoming a pastor and I'm even more sure that if you allow me to be Cynthia's boyfriend, I will never hurt her heart." Pastor Dawson was caught off guard by Elijah's response. He locked eyes with Elijah as he sat down his glass of Crown Royal. He wanted to intimidate Elijah into looking away or to drop his head, but Elijah did neither.

"You got some heart son! I may not like your wishes, but I gotta respect them because you came to me like a man. If you're willing to show me that you're committed to becoming a great pastor and businessman, and I'll teach you everything there is about running a successful church. First thing you must never do is tell a soul any of my personal business. And maybe, just maybe, I'll allow you to be the man for my Cynthia." Pastor Dawson stood up from his seat and reached his hand out for Elijah to shake it.

"Thanks sir! I won't let you down!" Elijah happily shook Pastor Dawson's hand. Pastor Dawson smiled.

"I know you won't son. And from here on out, call me Pops! You got a ride home?"

"Yeah Pops. My brother is outside waiting on me."

"Here's my numbers. I'll see you here on Tuesday at 5 pm." Pastor Dawson handed Elijah his business card.

"Okay Pops! I got you." With that said, Elijah left out of Pastor Dawson's presence.

"Damn Shawty! What the fuck took you so long? I been out this bitch for damn near a hour!" James Jr. said as soon as Elijah got into his car. He had only been waiting on Elijah for five minutes.

"My bad, bruh!" Elijah apologized.

"Yeah, you damn right, yo bad. Nigga, I got money waiting on me!" James Jr. fired up his blunt as he pulled off from the church parking lot, making the tires screech on his Cutlass Oldsmobile. He drove to the Econo Lodge Motel on Old National Road where he had been staying at for the past few months since Elijah had found his weed stash at his mama's house. James Jr. was trapping out of the motel like it was the Carter.

"I'll be right back, Shawty!" James Jr. told Elijah when he got out of his car to run inside his motel room. As soon as James Jr. went into his room, the Red Dogs pulled into the motel parking lot and raided the motel. The Narcs caught James Jr. with a big Eight (4 and ½ ounces of crack) of crack and a semi-automatic handgun in his possession. Elijah watched the police load James Jr. into the back of a police cruiser. That was the last time Elijah saw his brother for a long time.

For the next four years, Elijah spent damn near every day with Pastor Dawson learning everything that was to be learned about being a pastor and businessman. Or he was with Cynthia, falling deeper in love with her. Elijah constantly proclaimed his love for Cynthia. He told her he was ready to marry her so that they could spend the rest of their lives together. The only problem was that Cynthia had her guard up on Elijah for a reason unknown to Elijah.

Sinful Behavior

Until one day while they were watching a movie, he asked her why she wouldn't submit to his love.

"Cynt, baby, why don't you wanna marry me?" Elijah asked as they sat on the couch watching Menace to Society. Cynthia looked Elijah in his eyes and took a deep breath.

"I don't wanna get hurt like my mother. I know you know about my fathers' infidelities, so don't play stupid!" Elijah knew exactly what Cynthia was talking about. He sat up straight on the couch.

"Baby, I have nothing to do with what your father has going on. I'd never cheat on you or hurt you." Elijah pleaded to Cynthia.

"You say that now, Elijah. But what about in a few years when you become a well-known young pastor. Are you gonna be strong enough to be faithful to me or are you gonna be like your teacher?" Cynthia questioned Elijah. He grabbed her by her chin.

"Baby, I swear to you that you are all I ever will want or need. I love you with all my heart. Now and forever." Elijah reached into his pants pocket and pulled out a small black velvet box. Then he opened it. Cynthia smiled when she saw the beautiful diamond ring inside the box. Elijah got down onto the floor and kneeled on one knee while he held the ring in front of him.

"Baby, will you marry me?" This was the first time Elijah had actually proposed to Cynthia.

"Yes, Elijah! I will marry you!" Cynthia's words made Elijah the happiest young man on earth.

The week after Elijah and Cynthia graduated High School they got married. Cynthia got pregnant a week later while they were on their honeymoon in Barbados. Nine months later she gave birth to their baby boy, Elijah Malikah Woods Jr. For the next two years, Elijah worked as Pastor Dawson's assistant and he attended Morehouse College, where he gained an associate degree in Business. The week after Elijah received his Associates Degree, Pastor Dawson told him he was ready to deliver the knowledge of God.

At twenty years old, Elijah preached his first sermon. The church went wild and Brenda cried as she listened to her baby boy deliver such a powerful message. Brenda couldn't be more proud of Elijah as she cried from happiness that he'd taken the same path as his father and become a preacher. That night became even more special

Sinful Behavior

because Elijah got Cynthia pregnant again and nine months later she gave birth to their daughter, Samantha.

When Cynthia got out of the hospital from having Samantha, Pastor Dawson and his wife Pam gave Cynthia their house. Pastor Dawson and Pam moved into a condo in the Buckhead area. Now with two kids, Cynthia's dreams and goals of becoming a traveling nurse would have to wait for a while. That summer after Pastor Dawson moved into the condo with his wife Pam, he had a stroke while he was driving and crashed into a brick wall which killed him upon impact. Knowing the real reason her husband had a stroke, Pam moved to Dallas, Texas immediately after the funeral to start a new life with her new young flame.

Surprised by Pastor Dawson's sudden death, the church board had to vote on who would be the next pastor of the church. With Deacon Jones having various health problems, the only two people left that were qualified for the position was Elijah and Karter Jones, who was the son of Deacon Jones. Karter told the church board that he wasn't ready to become the pastor, but he really didn't accept the position because he knew that his childhood friend's husband would need the job to support her and their kids. The board elected Elijah to be the pastor in charge of A New Ministry and he overbearingly accepted the job.

With Elijah always away from home, Cynthia had nothing to do but stay in the house to watch after the kids. Her body didn't bounce back like she planned for it to, like it did after she had Elijah Jr. After she gave birth to Samantha, Cynthia gained about forty pounds. She became very insecure of her body and for that reason, she even stopped going to church. After weighing 130 pounds for more than half of her life, it was almost impossible for Cynthia to adjust to weighing close to 180 pounds. Elijah's fat jokes didn't help Cynthia with her complex nor did his distance from her in the bedroom.

Four years after Cynthia had her last baby, she signed up for college and began pursuing her nursing career, since Elijah Jr. and Samantha both were in elementary school. Elijah had become very busy with the church and he rarely paid any attention to Cynthia or the kids. Of course, with him becoming a very popular young pastor in Atlanta, there were hundreds of women inviting Elijah to their homes for a special prayer service. Six years after becoming pastor at A New Life Ministry Church,

Sinful Behavior

Elijah started building a bigger church in Buckhead for the church to relocate to. The new church was planned to be twice the size as the building they were already in. Next, he moved Cynthia and the kids into a 1.8-million-dollar mansion-like home in the Stone Mountain area.

Standing six foot two, weighing two hundred pounds, brown-skinned with good hair, thick eyebrows and dimples, which all made women seem to fall on his married lap. At the age of thirty-five, Pastor Elijah Malikah Woods was on top of the world. His three-million-dollar church was almost paid for and his congregation was growing by the sermons. Both of his kids were in high school and his wife was a nurse. Elijah had it all. Or at least he thought he did.

CHAPTER TWO

Elijah has had his eyes on Tasha Caine for about two years. Ever since she moved back to Atlanta from Miami, where she went to college at and lived with her husband who's a doctor. Elijah was sitting in the pulpit the first day he saw her walk into the sanctuary with her mother, Coretta Caine. Tasha was sporting her natural hair in a bun with a Chinese bang that almost covered her eyes. The pink Kim Wooo pants suit she was wearing bear hugged her body, exposing her immaculate shape as she walked between the pews, stepping one Red Bottom at a time. That was the first time that Elijah had seen Tasha in over sixteen years. Elijah and Tasha had indulged in minor conversation as a youth, but nothing more than that because Cynthia had his full attention back then. But in the present-day Tasha was the apple in Elijah's eye and Cynthia was the last person on his mind. For the past year and a half, Elijah and Tasha had spoken a few times and had a few casual conversations, but things had never been taken any further between them. Reason being Elijah had a rule that he lived by when it came to the women of the church. If

Sinful Behavior

the woman initiates the come-on to him, then it's okay, but he couldn't be the one to approach the females. This was the first time Tasha had ever invited him to her mother's house for dinner. Tasha knew Elijah knew where Coretta's house was at because Elijah had been with Pastor Dawson when he had come over there in the past.

Elijah looked at the surveillance footage on the fifty-inch plasma TV that was mounted on the wall inside of his office and he saw the deacons leaving out of the church. He left out of his office and checked the entire church to make sure that it was empty. Afterwards he activated the alarm to the church and left out of the building. When he walked outside the parking lot was empty except for his Mercedes Benz G-Wagon truck and Deacon Jones' out of date Cadillac that he refused to get rid of. Karter got out of his Cadillac and popped the hood.

"Looks like the Caddy has finally gave up on you!" Elijah joked with Karter, who didn't see anything funny as he wiggled his battery cables.

"Damn! I sholl hate to admit it, but you might be right! Damn!" Karter wiped the sweat from his forehead as he went and sat inside the Caddy to try to start it, but it didn't make a sound.

"Yeah, it's over wit, bruh. Old Betsie is gone to the Cadillac afterlife." Elijah said and they both burst into laughter.

"Damn! Now I gotta bring out the McLaren."

"I don't know why you ain't been brought it out anyways."

"I didn't want to raise any eyebrows. Even though I make good money, I still don't wanna be sticking out. If someone on the outside looking in at me and you, they probably think that we are drug dealers or something of that sort." Karter explained as he closed the hood of the Cadillac then got inside of Elijah's G-Wagon.

"Bruh, they gonna think what they wanna think anyways. But on the real, I'm glad that you didn't bring it out cause you probably would've pulled my woman before I can get over to Mother Caine's house to eat dinner." Elijah pulled out of the church parking lot.

"I guess I'm eating dinner with y'all then, huh bruh!" Karter smiled.

"Hell nawl, where you goin?" Elijah's tone of voice got serious and Karter could tell that he was really feeling some type of way about Tasha.

Sinful Behavior

"Mane alright! Damn! Take me to the crib." Said Karter as he turned up the radio, which was playing Future and Drake's song "Used to This."

From a distance Elijah saw the light ahead of him on Main Street turn yellow so he started slowing down. Just then his phone began vibrating on his hip. He grabbed his phone and unlocked it. He saw that it was a Facebook message from Tasha and he excitedly opened the message.

"Aye bruh, watch out!" Karter screamed, but it was too late.

Boomp Ba Boomp Boom

"Oh shit! What was that, bruh?" Elijah was clueless to what he had run over as he pulled over to see.

"Nigga that was a person! You better pull off!" Karter knew that the person had to be hurt because he saw when they flipped over the SUV after they were hit.

"Damn! I can't pull off!" Elijah got out of the truck. Before he reached the rear of his truck, he saw the person that he hit laying in the middle of the street. Elijah slowly approached the body. Karter got out of the truck and ran up beside Elijah.

"Huuum! Hummghm!" The homeless looking man on the ground moaned from the pain he was feeling.

"Shit man! What am I gonna do? I just can't leave him here!" Elijah couldn't believe what had happened.

"I don't know bruh, but he looks like he is in bad shape!" Karter got closer to the man, trying to look at his face, but the hair on the man's face made it difficult to see his features.

"Excuse me, sir! Sir! Do you have a name?" Elijah asked the man, but he didn't reply. Elijah looked at Karter.

"Come on bruh! Help me put him in the truck." Elijah told Karter as he grabbed the man under his arm pits. Karter grabbed the man by his feet, and they loaded the man into the back of Elijah's Benz truck. The smell of cheap wine, cigarettes and some other horrible stench immediately filled the inside of the truck as soon as the man was inside the truck.

"Huumghh! Humgrrh!" The man continued to moan in the back seat.

"He smells like shit!" Karter said as he rolled down his window. Elijah remained silent. All he could do was hope that the man in the back of him wasn't too badly hurt. She'll know what to do. Hell, she can even take him to the hospital she works at, thought Elijah as he drove to his house in Stone Mountain.

****

Sundays had become Cynthia's me-days since she was always at home alone. The kids were usually gone to their friends' house and Elijah was out being "Pastor Save The World." Three to four years ago Cynthia started buying sex toys since she wasn't getting the attention and affection she needed from her husband. It didn't take Cynthia long to learn how to please herself and that's how she spent most of her Sundays. Just like she was right now in her king-size bed, butt naked with her phone in her hand watching The Body XXX get dicked down by the porn star, Dr. Feel Good.

"Ooh, sii!" Cynthia moaned as she watched the porn video on her iPhone while she inserted the head of the six-inch dildo that she held in her hand inside of her tight, wet pussy. Her pussy stayed tight since the only time it got penetrated was when she pleased herself.

"Ehmm, ahh!" Cynthia fucked her pussy with the dildo to the same rhythm as Dr. Feel Good was fucking The Body XXX. It felt so good to Cynthia that she had to spread her thick thighs further apart and dig deeper into her soaking wet pussy. She was so far deep in her zone that she didn't hear the garage door open, nor did she hear the chime alert on the house alarm.

"Ahh, ah, oohh yesss!" Cynthia pounded away at her insides with the six-inch dildo.

"Bruh, do me a favor. Run upstairs and get Cynt for me. Tell her I said to hurry up and come down here." Elijah told Karter as they laid the man on the couch inside of the garage. Karter let loose of the man's feet and flew inside the house to go upstairs. When he didn't see Cynthia on the first level of the house, he ran upstairs to Elijah's bedroom and twisted the doorknob.

"Ahh siii, oohh, ah, ehmm!" Karter couldn't believe his eyes as he watched Cynthia bring herself to an orgasm with a dildo. Got damn! She is so fuckin' thick and pretty. Her pussy is so fuckin' wet. Her feet are gorgeous, thought Karter who was amazed by the scene he

Sinful Behavior

was watching. Cynthia would've seen Karter step into the bedroom, but she had her eyes glued to her phone.

"Cynthia, Elijah wants you in the garage. It's urgent!" Cynthia damn near jumped under the bed when she looked up and saw Karter. She was so ashamed and embarrassed. Karter couldn't help but wonder what Cynthia tasted like.

"Don't worry. I didn't see anything. I won't say a word." Karter promised then he left out of the bedroom with his brain running wildly about Cynthia. Damn! Why the fuck did I have to see that? She creamed that damn dildo. Fuck thought Karter as he walked downstairs to the garage.

"Hell, yeah baby, a fuckin' bum. I get so tired of they asses. I had one guy walk up to me a few days ago when I walked out of the church, asking me for change. I told him to get his smelly ass away from my church before I called the cops. Give me about an hour and I'll be pulling up beautiful!" Elijah hung up his phone.

"What did Cynt say?" Elijah asked Karter as soon as he got off the phone with Tasha.

"She's on the way down!" Karter couldn't believe the words Elijah had just said out of his mouth. This dude has to be stupid. He is chasing all these women, but he has a thick, beautiful woman like Cynthia upstairs, who has to fuck herself because he won't give her any attention, thought Karter shaking his head.

Oh my God! How long was he standing there? I hope he doesn't tell Elijah. Oh God, thought Cynthia as she walked downstairs to see what Elijah wanted with her that was so urgent that he sent another man into their bedroom. After seeing nobody was on the first level of the house, Cynthia walked to the garage.

"What's going on?" Cynthia asked when she saw the homeless looking man laying on the couch, while she tried to prevent from looking in Karter's direction.

"I hit this bum on the way to take Karter home!" Said Elijah.

"So, what do you want me to do, Elijah? Why didn't you take him to the hospital?" Asked Cynthia.

"'Cause maybe I want you to take him to the hospital. That's why got damn it! I have a second service that I have to attend." Elijah screamed and Karter looked at him like he had lost his mind. Cynthia teared up immediately.

"Sniff, sniff! Okay. I'll take him to the hospital!" A tear fell from Cynthia's eye. Karter couldn't believe how Elijah was treating Cynthia.

"Nah Shawty. You can't send her to the hospital with this man that nobody knows. Give me the keys to your other car. I'll take him my damn self. What the fuck, Elijah? You trippin' Shawty!" Karter was mad as hell.

"Thanks, bruh!" Elijah took his car keys off the key chain and gave them to Karter.

"Let me hurry up and freshen up so I can make it to this service." Elijah dashed into the house and went upstairs to his room. The distinct smell of Cynthia's pussy filled his nose as soon as he walked into the bedroom. He looked on the bed and saw Cynthia's toy box. She better keep fuckin' herself 'cause I don't want any of it, thought Elijah as he stripped out of his clothes to get in the shower.

"Come here! Stop crying Cynt!" Karter stood up from his seat and took Cynthia into his arms.

"Sniff, hum, hum!" Cynthia cried on Karter's shoulder. Karter couldn't help but notice how soft Cynthia was. Visions of her stroking her pussy with the dildo flooded his mind and he found his little man coming to life. Karter let go of Cynthia and backed away from her.

"Get you some rest. It'll be okay, Cynt!" Karter watched Cynthia tuck her chin into her chest and walk into the house. Damn, thought Karter as he watched Cynthia's ass sway from side to side.

"Come on buddy! Let's get you to the hospital." Karter grabbed the man by the shoulder.

"Urghh, hmm!" The man grunted from the pain as he got up off the couch.

Karter drove to Grady Hospital since it was closer to his home. He took the man inside of the ER. The man was moving better but Karter could tell that the man was in severe pain by all the grunting and moaning he was doing. Karter realized that the man only made sounds since they picked him up off the ground. The man had not said one word, only sounds.

"What can I help you with?" The receptionist at the window asked Karter and the man. The man didn't say anything. He pointed to the woman's pen and paper. She slid it to him, and he began writing. I got hit by a car. I

Sinful Behavior

think my ribs are broken. My name is Thomas Clemons. I can't talk, but I do understand everything that you say. Thomas slid the receptionist the note. Damn, so dude can't talk! Oh shit, thought Karter when he read the note that Thomas gave the receptionist.

"Here. Fill out these papers!" She handed Thomas a clipboard with a few papers to fill out, but she had her eyes on Karter as she smiled seductively at him and popped the gum in her mouth loudly. Thomas quickly filled out the forms and handed her back the clipboard.

"Okay. Grab a seat and wait till your name is called." She instructed Thomas.

Ma'am, if you don't mind, could I borrow a pen and a piece of paper so I can communicate with my friend?" Karter smiled at the fat, black woman wearing the bright red lipstick who was the receptionist.

"You can have whatever you want, Handsome!" She wrote her phone number on the sheet of paper then handed it to Karter along with a pen. When Karter reached for the items, she quickly rubbed his hand.

"Thank you Beautiful!" Karter smiled then he and Thomas took a seat. Karter began writing as soon as he sat down. Are you ok? I'm sorry about what happened, wrote Karter then he passed the pen and paper to Thomas so he could respond. Yeah, I'm fine and your apology is accepted and I can hear you I just can't talk, Thomas replied. "What happened to your voice? Why can't you talk?" Karter asked, curious as to why Thomas couldn't talk. I ate the wrong pussy. LOL! Wrote Thomas and Karter looked at him like he was crazy. Thomas started writing again. No real talk when I found my wife and kids dead, I screamed so loud that I exploded my voice box. Thomas looked at Karter, who was shocked. Thomas started writing again. That's the same reason I look, smell and live the way I live right now. After I lost my family years ago, I gave up on life. A tear fell from Thomas's eye as he thought about the horrific scene of what happened.

"Damn, I'm sorry to hear that!" Karter saw the pain that revealed itself in Thomas's eyes. Karter wondered if he could help Thomas recover from the loss that he's suffered from.

"Thomas Clemons!" The nurse yelled. Thomas got up and walked to the back with her.

While Karter sat in the lobby area waiting on Thomas, his mind went all over the place, but the thought

Sinful Behavior

of Cynthia stayed in place and wouldn't move. Karter and Elijah had become friends when Elijah first became a member at A New Life Ministry. Karter's father, Deacon Jones, was Pastor Dawson's right-hand man, therefore it was only natural for Elijah and Karter to become friends. Karter and Cynthia had always had a brother and sister type of relationship because they were basically raised together in church. That is why it hurt Karter to see Cynthia cry from the way Elijah was treating her. Even though Cynthia is a grown woman with two kids and sixty pounds bigger than she was in high school, in Karter's eyes she was still the beautiful nerdy girl with glasses that had the heart of an angel. To see Cynthia in bed with her legs spread eagle as she inserted a toy dick in and out of her wet pussy only opened up a new door leading Karter into a different direction. No matter how hard Karter tried to think of something else, the scene of Cynthia creaming the dildo as she moaned from pleasure, wouldn't escape his mind. Being a single bachelor with no kids didn't help the situation either. Karter had plenty of women, but it was as if none of them had the chemistry he was looking for. Plus, a lot of the females that he had encountered were either Elijah's throwaways or they only wanted to be friends with Karter just to get closer to Elijah. Even though Karter was a successful foreign car salesman and owned a condo in downtown Atlanta, it was if he was always played second to Elijah.

"Mr. Clemons will be fine in a few days. All he needs is a little rest. He has a couple bruised ribs, but with the proper rest, he'll be like new in a few days. I gave him a prescription for the pain." The doctor told Karter when he walked Thomas out to the lobby.

"Okay Doc! Thanks!" Karter and Thomas left the hospital and went to Wal-Mart. He took Thomas inside to buy him underclothes, cheap cell phone, toiletries, shoes, clothes and some food. Once the prescription was filled, they left Wal-Mart. Karter took Thomas to Days Inn and bought him a room for a week. Karter helped Thomas carry his belongings into the room. I swear this guy looks familiar, thought Karter before he walked out of the room. Thomas grabbed him by the arm, then he took the paper and pen out of his pocket and started writing. Thanks for everything lil bro. I'm gonna clean myself up. If you know anybody who needs a good worker, I'm the man for the job. I'm the jack-of-all-trades. Thomas passed the note to Karter. Karter read it then looked at Thomas and nodded his head.

Sinful Behavior

"We can use a janitorial worker at the church. I'll see you in a few days if you really bout what you talking bout. I'll be here Wednesday at four o'clock to pick you up. Activate your phone and save my number." Karter gave Thomas a business card then he pulled three blue hundred-dollar bills from his wallet and handed them to Thomas. Thomas released a tear from his eye as he picked up the pen to write. Thanks so much! I owe you dearly lil bro! I'll be waiting on you to pick me up Wednesday. Karter read the note.

"Bet! I'm out! I'll see you Wednesday!" Karter left the hotel feeling good that he was able to help someone in need as he drove home. When he pulled up at home, he realized that Elijah hadn't called. Dude really on some trip shit, thought Karter as he walked into his condo.

Karter took a shower and when he got out, he put on some Jordan gym shorts with the matching flip flops. Karter grabbed a Redd's Strawberry Ale from out of the fridge then went and took a seat on his black leather Ralph Lauren sectional. He took a swig from his Ale as he opened his phone. Sitting his Ale down on the hand-crafted mahogany table which sat in front of the sectional, Karter decided to grab the remote to his 84-inch HD flat screen that was mounted into the wall and he turned on VH1. Karter checked his IG messages, then he went to Facebook. For some reason he wanted to see Cynthia's face. Scrolling on Cynthia's page gave Karter the urge to want to inbox her, but he fought against the thought. He checked the messages in his inbox. There were five females in his inbox trying to get in touch with Elijah and there were ten females in his inbox who were trying to get with him, but Elijah had already fucked them. When will I be the first choice, thought Karter as he ran his fingers through his long dreads that stopped past his shoulders.

CHAPTER 3

Ever since Elijah ate dinner with Tasha, he couldn't think about anything or anyone else. Tasha had him hooked and he had not even kissed her yet. Her attitude, her smell, her shape, her conversation, her everything had Elijah fucked up in the head. He hadn't spoken one word to Cynthia since he ate the special spaghetti Tasha fed him at Mother Caine's house Sunday. Wednesday came and Elijah was supposed to be at church an hour early to meet Karter and Thomas, plus it was Bible study night, but Tasha had called at two p.m. and told him she wanted to go to the movies at five o'clock. Elijah changed his entire schedule for Tasha without thinking twice.

Karter's Cadillac was still at the church when Karter and Thomas pulled into the church parking lot. Karter couldn't help but to think about his father, Deacon Jones, who had died seven years earlier from a heart attack. His father gave him the Fleetwood Cadillac when he was fifteen, that's why Karter loved his Caddy so much. Thomas saw that Karter was in a daze as he looked at the

Cadillac. Thomas sent a message to Karter's phone asking him who's car it was.

"That's my old Caddy. It quit on me Sunday!" Karter said wondering if he should get the Caddy towed home or to the shop. Thomas messaged Karter again telling him to let him take a look at the Caddy. Karter reached in the cup holder and handed Thomas the keys. Thomas got out of the car and went and attended to the Lac. Elijah pulled up seconds later. He got out of his truck wearing Louis Vuitton from head to toe. He even had on a platinum chain with a nice sized diamond flooded cross on it. If you didn't know any better when you saw Elijah, you would think he was a "Dope Man" rather than a pastor.

Vrrroooom

"Oh shit!" Karter said as he jumped out of the car when he heard the Caddy crank up. Thomas got out of the Caddy smiling and shut the hood.

"You fixed it! Thanks, Bruh!" Karter dapped Thomas up.

"Who is he Bruh? I thought you said the guy I ran over was with you for the job." Elijah didn't recognize Thomas since he'd cleaned himself up.

Sinful Behavior

"This is him! His name Thomas!"

"Oh! You clean up pretty good for a bum!" Spat Elijah as he looked Thomas up and down. If looks could kill, Elijah would've been dead ten times because Thomas had murder written all over his face. What is dude's problem, thought Karter, not believing Elijah's harsh choice of words.

"I'm gonna take your car to your house since the Caddy crunk up." Karter told Elijah.

"Kool! The garage opener is on the visor. Show him his work detail. He does know he'll have to become a member of the church, doesn't he? And he can't be running around here stankin and lookin' rough!" Elijah was persistent with the bullshit.

"Bruh, he knows all that already!" Karter got mad.

"Well, I'm out! Either you or one of the other deacons can handle Bible study, can't you? I gotta movie date with Tasha to see the early show. She's playing real hard bruh." Elijah gave Karter some dap then he jumped into his truck and pulled off. This nigga losing his fuckin' mind behind this bitch and he ain't smelled the pussy yet, thought Karter as he watched Elijah pull off.

Michael "Oodoo" Smith

"My bad for the way____" Karter started apologizing, but Thomas waved his hand and shook his head, telling Karter to stop. Thomas pointed to Karter then to himself and did a thumbs up sign. Then he pointed in the direction Elijah drove off in and he threw up his middle finger. Karter burst into laughter.

"Come on! Let's go inside so I can show you around." Karter took Thomas into the church to show him his work details and where the supplies were located. As soon as Thomas stepped foot into the church, he was amazed at how luxurious the church was.

****

"Mom, you told me that I could go to the movies tonight with Josh." Fifteen-year-old Samantha flopped down on the couch, mad that her mother had lied to her.

"I told you if your father met Josh by today, then y'all could go to the movies!" Cynthia pleaded her case.

"How is Josh gonna meet somebody that nobody including his wife and kids ever knows where he is at?" Samantha had a point. Cynthia had no comeback for Samantha. She called Elijah's phone, but she got no answer. Cynthia called again, but this time Elijah's phone

Sinful Behavior

went straight to the voicemail. Samantha looked at her mother and shook her head. She hated how naïve her mother was for her father. Cynthia looked at her phone like she was dialing the wrong number. She took a deep breath.

"Okay, Sammie! Go get ready and call your date. I'll take y'all to the seven o'clock show."

"Yes! Thanks Mommy! You're the best!" Samantha jumped up and hugged Cynthia, then she ran upstairs to her room to get ready.

Cynthia repeatedly called Elijah's phone over and over, but it went straight to the voicemail box every time. Maybe he's having Bible study or something, thought Cynthia as she sat her phone down. An hour later Cynthia was dropping off Samantha at the movies for her first date.

"I'll be out here at 9:15 to pick y'all up." Cynthia told Samantha and Josh.

"Okay Mom! We'll see you then." Samantha and Josh jumped out of the car and walked up to the movie entrance because there was a fifteen-car line and Cynthia was near the back of the line. Cynthia smiled as she watched Samantha and Josh enter the movies but what she saw come out of the exit door crushed her heart. Cynthia's heart stopped beating as she watched Elijah come out of the movies holding hands with Tasha. Cynthia hadn't seen Elijah as happy as he seemed to be with Tasha since the day, he preached his first sermon.

BEEP BEEP BEEP

The cars behind Cynthia were blowing their horns for Cynthia to move forward, but she was frozen by the defeat of her emotions as she watched Elijah open the door to his truck for Tasha to get in.

KNOCK KNOCK

"Ma'am, could you move so we can pull up?" The lady said standing outside of Cynthia's window. Cynthia pulled away in tears. She cried all the way home. She felt like her heart had been put into a blender and gotten pureed. When she pulled into the garage at home, she just sat in the car, crying and praying that God would deliver her from her current situation.

****

After Bible study was over, Thomas trailed Karter to take Elijah's car home. Karter pushed the button on the garage opener and waited for the garage to open. Then he pulled in the garage next to Cynthia's car. Karter got out of the car. The headlights of the Cadillac were shining in the garage and the lights caused Karter to see Cynthia in her car. What the hell is she doing, thought Karter as he walked around to the driver's door of Cynthia's car. He leaned down to get a good look inside the car and saw that Cynthia was drowning in her own tears. He quickly opened the car door.

"Cynt, what's wrong?" With her face soaked in tears, Cynthia looked up at Karter.

"He, he, he wa, was at, th, the movies wi, wi, wit another woman!" Cynthia cried hysterically. Oh shit, thought Karter, knowing that Cynthia saw Elijah at the movies with Tasha. How fuckin' stupid could this nigga be, thought Karter.

"Come on Cynt, let's go inside." Karter grabbed Cynthia by her arm, slightly pulling for her to get out of the car. She didn't resist his pull. Cynthia got out of the car and fell into Karter's chest. Karter put his arms around her and gave her a hug.

"It's gonna be okay! You just need some rest." Karter let go of his embrace on Cynthia and led her into the house, upstairs to her bedroom being her support system the whole way there. He didn't take his arm from around her until they reached the bedroom.

"Just pray about it and everything will be okay!" Karter encouraged Cynthia as she walked into her bedroom. Cynthia turned around and stepped back up to the bedroom doorway, getting close to Karter. She was so close that Karter could smell her mint breath. Cynthia looked deep into Karter's eyes.

"I've already prayed, Karter. Then you showed up!" A lump formed in Karter's throat. He was paralyzed by Cynthia's remark. Cynthia placed her hands onto Karter's shoulders. Then she stood on her tippy toes and kissed Karter on the lips.

"Uhhmm!" Cynthia moaned as she stuck her tongue inside of Karter's mouth. Karter didn't resist, but he willingly entangled his tongue with Cynthia's and followed her as she back peddled to the bed. They never broke their kiss as Cynthia laid on the bed and Karter laid on top of her.

"We can't do this, Cynthia." Karter broke their kiss and tried to raise up, but Cynthia pulled him back downward.

Sinful Behavior

"Make love to me, Karter!" Cynthia slipped her hand in Karter's jeans and grabbed a hold of his small package.

"No! I can't!" Karter forcefully snatched Cynthia's hand out of his jeans and got up from atop of her.

BEEP BEEP BEEP

Fuck, thought Karter, knowing the Caddy's horn when he heard it. He walked out of the bedroom and hurried down the stairs into the garage. As soon as he stepped foot into the garage he was met by Elijah.

"What's up, Bruh?" Karter said keeping his cool.

"Nothin' bruh! How was Bible study?" Elijah closed the door to the house so nobody on the inside could hear their conversation.

"Oh, it was good!"

"You can go ahead and get with Cynthia now bruh. Tasha got me gone, bruh." Karter was caught off guard by Elijah's statement.

"What?" Wrinkles spread across Karter's forehead.

- 55 -

"You can get your childhood sweetheart now. I don't ever want her no more!" Elijah said playfully, but Karter wasn't catching on to the joke.

"What you talking bout me and Cynthia?" Karter grew frustrated.

"I'm just playing with you, bruh. Why you so uptight, bruh?" Elijah heard the seriousness in Karter's tone of voice.

"Nothin' bruh. I gotta go. Thomas is in the car waiting on me." Karter needed to leave. His conscience was fuckin' with him bad.

"Aight, Shawty. I'll holler at you later!" What's wrong with him thought Elijah as he watched Karter walk out of the garage.

When Karter got into the car, Thomas was smiling. Karter reversed out of the driveway with his mind running. Thomas sent Karter a message on his phone. Karter looked at the message as he drove away from Elijah's house. You got lipstick on your lips, fuck, thought Karter as he flopped down his visor to look in the mirror.

"Ain't nothing on my lips!" Karter looked over at Thomas who was clutching his stomach laughing.

Sinful Behavior

"Yeah, you got me!" Damn, how does he know so damn much without me telling him anything, thought Karter as he drove to his condo. Twenty minutes later, they pulled into the parking garage at Karter's condo. Karter told Thomas he could keep the Caddy for transportation. Karter got out of the car to walk in his crib. Thomas slid over to the driver's seat and quickly texted Karter. Karter opened the message while he waited for the elevator. Thanks for the wheels, bro. That woman deserves a good man, not that clown that she's married to. I'll see you tomorrow boss man. Karter looked up from his phone and he saw Thomas throwing up the peace sign as he drove off. Damn, is it that obvious, thought Karter with a smile on his face.

****

"Yeah, bitch! After the movies were over, I made the pastor bring me straight home." Tasha told her roommate Leikei who was walking into the kitchen wearing nothing but a halter top and her panties. Leikei had bright yellow skin and she was thick as gumbo. She had slanted eyes, high cheek bones, a fat ass, bowlegs and a pretty smile.

"I can't believe you ain't gave that man none of that pussy yeat girl!" Said Leikei as she got a two liter of Dirty Sprite out of the freezer then poured them a cup.

"Bitch, he thinks I'm a good girl, so I'm gonna let him think just that. By the time he finds out the truth about me, he'll be so gone over a bitch that he won't care about nothing but being with me." Tasha took a sip from her cup.

"Bitch, does he know that you work at the club?"

"Hell nawl! He asked me what I did for money and I told him that my husband gives me an allowance till our divorce gets settled!" Tasha smiled.

"Oooh bitch, you wrong! You know damn well that you ain't got no husband. So, he actually thinks that you were in Miami with your husband the African doctor."

"Bitch! You know I'm Coretta Caine's daughter!" They both burst into laughter.

Tasha Caine was the worst type of woman that any man could run across. She knew how to persuade, neglect, run game, finesse and whatever else she needed to do to get a man's heart, mind, and pockets. Tasha was a direct descendant of her Mother Coretta Caine, who has never worked a job in her life, but has always been well taken

Sinful Behavior

care of by a man. The vicious Coretta taught Tasha the ropes at an early age. When Tasha was fourteen, Coretta sucked Pastor Dawson's dick in front of her, showing how to make the Pastor catch the Holy Ghost. On Tasha's eighteenth birthday, she started working at Blue Flame. Two years later she moved to Miami with a guy she met at the Blue Flame, who made it rain ten bands on her in a single night. Miami took Tasha by a storm. She found herself in a relationship with drug dealer after drug dealer for a ten-year period. While she bounced around to different clubs stripping. Unfortunately for Tasha, things didn't work out for her like she wanted them to and she was forced to move back to Atlanta after she had to testify on her boyfriend at his murder trial. Tasha's been back in Atlanta for the past two years, working at the Blue Ivory, an upscale gentlemen's club. Taking advice from her mother Coretta, Tasha went to church and began to get the attention of Pastor Elijah Woods, protégé of Pastor Dawson who paid Coretta's bills till he took his very last breath.

"Bitch, I already know you gonna eat his ass and fuck his head up for sure!" Leikei said smiling.

"And you already know it Boo!" Tasha sipped her drink. Bitch tongue gonna fall out her mouf the way

Ralphy fat ass say she be stickin' her tongue in his ass, thought Leikei as she turned up her cup of Dirty Sprite.

"Oh yeah! Ralphy called my phone looking for you. He said Dr. Feel Good comin' to town to do a live show and he wants you to go with him." Leikei informed Tasha.

"Hell nawl! I can't chance being seen with Ralphy fat greasy ass while I got Elijah Woods on my line!" Tasha shook her head no. She had a mission to complete and she wasn't about to let anyone, or anything interfere with that. Tasha knew that Elijah wasn't being satisfied at home, therefore he was fooling around with random women, but she was about to fix all that, 'cause she was about to convince Elijah to divorce his wife and marry her.

****

It was time for Cynthia to go pick up Samantha and her date from the movies, but she didn't feel like reliving that moment when she saw Elijah come out of the movies smiling, holding hands with the daughter of the woman that her father was madly in love with for years. Thanks to Karter, who she couldn't get off her mind, Cynthia felt there was no need to say anything about what she saw. She made her mind up that she was calling a divorce lawyer the next morning. She was not gonna be stupid for Elijah any longer. He has proven to her that he is the least bit interested in the family he has at home.

Cynthia went to Elijah's study office and twisted the knob, but the door was locked. Why does he have the door locked, thought Cynthia, but then the door came open.

"Yeah! What's up?" Elijah asked her.

"Samantha and her friend Josh have to be picked up from the movies at 9:15. Can you go and get them? I don't feel too well. Cynthia began seeing visions of Elijah and Tasha walking out of the movies, holding hands as she stood in front of Elijah. Her palms got sweaty and the hair on the back of her neck stood up.

"Nah! I'm busy working on the sermon for Sunday. It's Remembrance Day so I need for you to be there!"

"I don't wanna come to church Sunday!" Cynthia argued.

"But you don't have a fuckin choice! Do you?" Elijah's voice got very stern and meaningful. Somehow Cynthia thought about the fact that Karter would be at church and a smile spread across her face.

"Okay, Elijah. I'll be there!" Cynthia left Elijah standing there and she walked downstairs to the theater room where she knew Elijah Jr. would be at with one of his homeboys from school, watching a movie. The theater room was nice. It had a 120-inch projector screen on the wall, and four rows of leather recliner chairs, four in each row. Cynthia opened the door and stuck her head inside. The lights were off, but there were some music videos playing on the screen. That must be Jr., thought Cynthia when she saw somebody laid back in a recliner.

"Jr.!" Cynthia yelled loud enough to be heard over the music. The guy in the recliner turned around, but it wasn't Jr. Jr. raised his head up from out the guy's lap. He had slob around his mouth.

"Oh my God!" Cynthia yelled but no words came out of her mouth. Elijah Jr. got up from his seat and ran up to his mother.

"Mom, I'm sorry! I'm sorry you had to find out like this, mom!" Jr. wiped his face as he apologized. He didn't know what to do, but who would? My son is gay, thought Cynthia, not knowing what to say, but knowing in her heart that she should have been known about her child's sexuality. She knew she had been slackin' as a parent.

Sinful Behavior

Cynthia stood with her mouth gaped open while her brain tried to calculate what she had just seen.

"Mom, please don't tell dad, please mom!" Elijah Jr. begged. He stood six-foot-one with good hair, a muscular body and he was as handsome as he could be. But yet he was sweet as cotton candy.

"You know what, Jr.? I'm not gonna tell him anything. You are! I'll let you know when you should introduce your friend right to your father. Okay!" Jr. couldn't believe how well Cynthia was taking things.

"Okay! Thanks Mom! I love you!" Jr. said smiling.

"Now go get your sister from the movies!" Cynthia walked up stairs to her bedroom feeling emotionally stronger and more mentally aware than she had ever been due to the fact that she knew more about her surroundings and loved ones. Even though it hurt Cynthia to find out that her son was gay, she still loved him no matter what. What a hell of a day, thought Cynthia as she climbed into her bed.

CHAPTER 4

Karter opened his eyes from the sound of his 6:00 AM alarm. He rose up in the bed to get ready for work. Karter grabbed his phone from the nightstand. When he opened his screen, he had a picture message from Thomas. Damn, thought Karter when he saw how Thomas had the Caddy looking like new money. Karter was about to set his phone down, but five Facebook message alerts came in. Who is this, wondered Karter.

"Look at this pretty ass pussy here! Got Damn!" Was all that Karter could say as he read the message under the pictures from Cynthia: Good morning we are on our way to work and we wanted you to know that we were thinking about you. Love Cint and Miss Kitty!

Wow, Cint really wants to fuck wit me, thought Karter as he examined the pics again. He found himself getting aroused. I should send her a picture of my dick, thought Karter, but when he pulled down his shorts and stared at his four inches of hardness, he quickly changed his mind. Karter got out of bed, showered and got ready

Sinful Behavior

for work. He thought about Cynthia all day as he worked. At lunch time he sent her a dozen red roses to her job. When Cynthia received the roses, she melted like some ice cream on a hot summer day after she read the card inside the roses that said from her secret lover. Cynthia called Karter and thanked him for the roses. She asked him to meet her at Pappadeux when he got off work and he agreed.

Karter pulled up at the restaurant at 4:00PM sharp. As soon as he stepped into the restaurant, he saw Cynthia sitting alone in a booth. Karter nervously looked around to see if there was anyone inside the restaurant that he knew as he walked towards Cynthia, who started smiling when she saw him headed in her direction.

"What's up beautiful?" Karter said as he slid into her booth next to Cynthia. Cynthia was so overwhelmed that she couldn't resist touching Karter's dreads.

"Karter I can't stop thinking about you!" Cynthia admitted as she stared into Karter's eyes. Then she leaned in and kissed him on the lips. Karter was startled by Cynthia's bold actions. He had to regain his composure when she broke their kiss. Every time Cynthia kissed Karter, he felt a tide of sensual pleasure rush through his body, but at the very moment his nervousness was getting the best of him.

"Damn, Cynthia! I, I'm speechless! Like I mean I like you too, but don't you think that we're wrong for being here together?" Karter's conscious was bothering him and he felt like he was betraying Elijah. Cynthia couldn't believe how extremely scary Karter was acting as she watched him constantly scan the restaurant. Her smile was replaced by a frown.

"Let me out!" Cynthia grabbed her purse and keys to leave. Karter slid out of the booth to allow Cynthia to slide out. She slid out and looked Karter in the eyes.

"When you figure out that Elijah doesn't give a fuck about no one, but himself. Then you contact me!" Cynthia stormed away. Karter stood there looking stupid. He couldn't believe Cynthia's new attitude. It was like she was a whole totally different person than the person he grew up knowing. Karter sat down in the booth and when the waitress came, he ordered a grilled steak plate. When he got done eating, he left the restaurant to go to the church for basketball practice.

****

Sinful Behavior

"Girl, Pastor Woods is so damn fine! Watch when he make a basket, he gonna look over here at us. I heard that he likes his women young." Thomas heard one of the young ladies sitting in the bleachers say as he dumped the trash cans in the gym. He watched Elijah shake and bake the guy guarding him with a crossover then go to the hole and lay the ball up for two points. It seemed like as soon as Elijah's feet touched the ground after he scored, he looked over at the young ladies sitting in the bleachers. Thomas shook his head in disbelief that Elijah was trying to showboat for some girls who looked to be no older than eighteen.

"Girl Jamal wants to talk to you!" Thomas heard one of the girls say as she handed her friend the phone.

"What Jamal?" Tara said into the phone when she got it from Kesha.

"Yeah, you can come so I can help you with your homework, but you know I'm a virgin so don't try to play me like you be doing those other THOTS!" Tara informed Jamal.

"Okay my address is 1402 Skyline Lane." Thomas took out his phone and put in the info he had just heard. That may be very helpful real soon, thought Thomas.

"Ball game!" Elijah yelled after he shot the ball. Everybody watched as the ball floated in the air.

SWISH!

Elijah hit the winning shot. Then he gave his teammates a high five.

"Well look what the wind blew in!" Elijah threw the basketball at Karter. Karter threw the ball back at Elijah.

"What's up big bruh!" Karter said to Thomas as they gave each other dap, but they were suddenly interrupted.

"Why don't you come out here, so I can give you this work while Thomas goes and washes the Benz Truck for me. My keys are over there inside that black Nike gym bag." Elijah pointed towards the gym bag. I can't stand this weak ass dude, thought Thomas.

"I'll catch up wit you later bro!" Karter told Thomas before he went onto the court.

Thomas went to the gym bag and got out Elijah's keys. Knowing that Elijah was busy, Thomas took the opportunity to go to the Pastor's office to snoop around.

Sinful Behavior

Damn, thought Thomas when he opened the door of Elijah's office. Looks more like a damn Penthouse rather than an office, thought Thomas right before he noticed a stack of money sitting on Elijah's desk. Thomas took half of the money and stuffed it into his pocket. Then he looked around the office some more. He saw a clothes hamper in the rear of the room which was filled with clothes. Thomas grabbed the trash bag out of the trash can and threw some of Elijah's clothes inside the bag. These have to be the loudest shoes I've ever seen, thought Thomas when he laid eyes on a pair of mustard yellow Mauri Gators sitting under Elijah's desk. Thomas put the shoe in the bag with the clothes then he quickly left out of the office, locking the door behind him.

****

Cynthia sat inside her hot tub soaking, trying to relax her mind that Karter had invaded. She had drunk almost the whole bottle of Stella Rosa that she had gotten from the store before she made it home. Cynthia sipped from a flute while she listened to Keith Sweat's "Sweat Hotel" on the radio.

"Saturday night we have something real special for you ladies coming to the InterContinental in Buckhead!

Porn Star Dr. Feel Good will be here in the house, live and in action. So, ladies be there and maybe you'll be lucky enough to get your wildest fantasy fulfilled by the one and only Dr. Feel Good!" Cynthia's pussy damn near jumped out of the hot tub when she heard Dr. Feel Good's name on the radio. I got be there, thought Cynthia. Then the bedroom door opened, and Elijah walked in. He looked at Cynthia and shook his head when he saw the empty wine bottle on the side of the hot tub.

"So that's what you do in your spare time! Fill your body with that poison!" Grouched Elijah.

"I____" Cynthia began saying.

"Shut up Cynthia! I don't wanna hear nothing you got to say!" Elijah went in the bathroom to take a shower.

"Hmmm! Then I won't bother to tell you anything! Find it out yourself, just like I had too!" Cynthia grinned then she turned up her glass of wine as she thought about the fact that Elijah's words didn't hurt her feelings.

Elijah texted Tasha while he sat on the toilet taking a shit. He wanted Tasha so bad that the sight of Cynthia was beginning to make his skin crawl.

Sent – I can't take it any longer baby! I need you!

Sinful Behavior

Rcvd – I want you too, but what about your wife

Sent – Baby don't worry about her! I'm not worried about your husband

Rcvd – me and my husband don't live together Elijah

Sent – so what do you want me to do

Rcvd – I saw a condo for sale

Sent – What are you saying Tasha?

Rcvd – I want us to start our own family

Sent – I got you beautiful. Can I see you tonight?

Rcvd – I would love to, but I know what it would lead to

Sent – What's wrong with that

Rcvd – Goodnight Handsome!

Sent – Baby I need to see you

Elijah sat on the toilet for five minutes waiting on Tasha to reply, but she never did. Elijah took a deep breath in disappointment. Then he wiped his ass and got into the shower.

Michael "Oodoo" Smith

****

Tasha probably would've entertained Elijah's wishes, but his timing was off, that's why she ended the texting session. She hit her blunt of Spaceship Fuel two more times, then her and Leikei got out of the car to go into the Blue Ivory so they could go to work. Tasha knew that Ralphy the club manager was gonna be on the bullshit because she hadn't returned any of his phone calls.

"Hey baby let me hit you back! I gotta handle this business that just walked into my office! Well if it ain't my lying ass fuck buddy Tash Tash!" Ralphy the short black fat club manager with a gap in his mouth got happy when he saw Tasha walk into his small office.

"Ralphy, baby you know I've been busy helping my mama!" Tasha tried to "G" Ralphy, but he wasn't goin.

"Bitch you got me fucked up shawty! See you think you slick! You know Lil Baby, Gunna and Young Thug gonna be in here tonight!" Ralphy laughed. Tasha knew he was right.

"But you won't be getting on my stage……. Unless you eat this ass in front of Leikei! Yea, I want my lil sista to see how nasty you can really get!" Ralphy smiled.

Sinful Behavior

Tasha's stomach turned ten cartwheels. How did I end up eating this fat funky ass bitch ass in the first place, thought Tasha. Leikei couldn't believe how Ralphy put Tasha on the glass like he did. She couldn't believe that Tasha didn't come back.

"Baby for real! You gonna do me like this!" Tasha pleaded.

"Damn right! I know dem bills due!" Ralphy said with a serious face. Tasha couldn't stoop so low to perform such an action in front of Leikei.

"Call me if you need me to come pick you up girl!" Tasha left out of Ralphy's office. She dialed Elijah's number before she made it out of the club. I gotta go ahead and hook this nigga like a fish tonight, thought Tasha as she listened to Elijah's phone while she walked to her car. Her car note was due on her Audi A8 and she needed to come with her half of the rent on the condo she shared with Leikei.

****

Elijah was sitting on the edge of the bed lotioning his body, damn near about to give in to getting into the hot tub with Cynthia when his phone began vibrating next to him. A smile spread across his face when he saw Tasha's name. He answered the phone without caring that Cynthia was only a few feet away from him.

"Hey, What's up?" Elijah tried to talk in a neutral tone of voice so that Cynthia wouldn't know whether he was talking to a male or female.

"Baby I tried to play hard, but I can't take it any longer. I want you Elijah!" Elijah couldn't believe his ears as he listened to Tasha while he looked at Cynthia whose eyes were staring at his mouth.

"I know! Me too! Let me get dressed and I'll call you back so we can come up with a solution!" Elijah kept his composure.

"Baby don't keep me waiting!" Tasha sounded like she was fiending for Elijah.

"I won't! I got you!" Elijah hung up his phone while he hid his excitement.

"I'm bout to go over to Karter's house for a while to go over some business. I'll be back later!" Elijah told Cynthia as he walked pass her on his way to his closet.

Sinful Behavior

"Oh okay! Samantha wants you to meet her friend tomorrow when she gets out of school and Junior said he has something very important to tell you!" Cynthia spoke lightly.

"I'll see what I can do! I have more important issues to deal with right now!" Elijah said with a slight attitude.

"Don't worry hubby I'll just take care of everything!" Elijah was so focused on getting to Tasha that he didn't catch on to the sarcasm in Cynthia's voice. This Tasha bitch really has my husband gone just like her mother had my daddy gone over her, thought Cynthia as she grabbed her phone from the side of the hot tub to text Karter. She was tipsy from the wine and just the sound of Karter's voice would do her some justice. Before she could start typing her text, a message came to her phone.

Rcvd – From KJ, just thinking about you

Cynthia smiled from ear to ear when she read Karter's message the she responded.

Sent – You've been on my mind all day. Can I call you

Rcvd – Sure baby

Cynthia watched as Elijah walked out of the bedroom dressed to impress in a Kim Woo linen outfit with a pair of brown Gucci loafers on his feet. Some business he's finna handle, thought Cynthia. As soon as she heard the garage door open then close, she called Karter.

"What's up beautiful?" Karter answered.

"You, handsome!" Cynthia smiled as she found herself feeling a little tingle between her thighs from Karter's voice.

"I'm sorry about earlier Cynt!"

"No need to apologize! I know this might be a difficult situation for you, but I've come to the realization that Elijah doesn't care about anyone but himself. Just like my daddy!" Karter was surprised at Cynthia's bold choice of words.

"Yeah, I hate to admit it, but you're right!"

"I wanna know something about you Karter!"

"What's up? Ask me anything!"

"Do you watch porn?"

"Ha! Yes, I do and what about you?"

"Haha! Real funny! You caught me doing me, remember!"

"How could I ever forget!" Karter laughed.

"I know right! I don't know if you're familiar with the Porn Star Dr. Feel Good, but he's gonna be in town with a few female porn stars Saturday at the InterContinental in Buckhead and I wanna go see him." Cynthia waited for Karter's response.

"Wow! Cynt, I don't know about that! Like there's no telling who will be there." Karter wasn't sure about the idea.

"You don't have to worry about anyone seeing us together, it's a masquerade. Women have to wear a negligee and the men can only wear some type of underwear!" Cynthia wanted to convince Karter, who thought about what she was saying for a moment before he responded.

"Okay! It's a date!" Karter agreed. Cynthia smiled from ear to ear.

"I can't wait to see you there!" Cynthia's voice was very seductive to Karter.

"Damn Cynt! You got me wanting you!" Karter admitted.

"I want you ten times more! Oh yeah Karter!"

"What's up baby?"

"Size doesn't matter to me as long as it's mines!" Cynthia hung up leaving Karter smiling and shaking his head at her statement.

****

Elijah knocked on the door of room 112 at the Westin. Then he noticed his wedding band, so he quickly took it off and put it in his pants pocket before Tasha answered the door. When the room door opened Elijah got paralyzed by Tasha's appearance. The powder blue see through negligee she was wearing left nothing to the imagination. Her dark brown nipples protruded through the material of the negligee. She wore her hair straight down her back with a Chinese bang.

"Are you gonna come in or are you gonna just stare at me crazy!" Tasha knew she had Elijah's full attention when his eyes floated to her hot red painted toes. She turned around and walked towards the bed giving each step she took extra emphasis by making her ass cheeks do the wave. Elijah walked into the room trying to keep his thoughts together, but he was unable to.

"Can I have a drink?" Elijah noticed a bottle of Patron sitting on the table next to the lamp. Hopefully a drink will calm my nerves, thought Elijah as he sat on the side of the bed.

"Baby relax, you can have whatever you want!" Tasha fixed Elijah a stiff shot of Tequila while he scooted back onto the bed getting comfortable. Elijah downed the Tequila as soon as Tasha handed him the cup. Tasha took off his shoes for him, then she climbed into the bed next to him and began unbuttoning his shirt.

For some unknown reason Elijah felt butterflies in his stomach. He had never felt the way he was feeling around any other woman. He had been with over a hundred women, but Tasha had him feeling like he was a little boy. Why am I so nervous? Mane let me get right, thought Elijah, then he stood up from the bed and stripped out of all of his clothing. Damn baby packin, thought Tasha as she stared at Elijah's half erect dick. She stood up from the bed and turned her back to Elijah.

"Help me out of this!" She instructed Elijah and he began slowly unsnapping the negligee she was wearing.

Tasha let the negligee fall to the floor then she turned around and pushed Elijah onto the bed. Turn this nigga out Tasha! Don't play with him! Tasha told herself as she crawled onto the bed and up to Elijah's face. While staring into Elijah's eyes Tasha connected her lips to his and then stuck her tongue into his mouth.

"Ehhhmmm!" Tasha moaned softly as their tongues wrestled. Elijah had never been kissed so freakishly by any other woman. Tasha ran her tongue across Elijah's teeth and gums while she explored his whole mouth with her tongue, then she broke their kiss.

"I love you, Elijah!" Tasha stared deep into Elijah's eyes.

"I love you too, Tasha!" Replied Elijah knowing that he didn't a woman could make him fall in love with her in such a short period of time. Tasha kissed him on the lips then she softly pecked down to his neck, down his chest and she didn't stop until she made it right below his navel. Tasha looked Elijah in his eyes while she grabbed his thick, long, hard dick with her soft hands and put it into her warm mouth without breaking eye contact with him. Elijah's toes immediately began twinkling from the warmth of Tasha's mouth.

Sinful Behavior

"Siii baby!" Elijah moaned as he placed his hand on top of Tasha's head. Tasha cupped Elijah's balls with her free hand and began bobbing up and down on his dick head to a nice slow rhythm while she massaged his balls at the same time.

Gugh Gugh Gugh Gugh Gugh Gugh

"Damn baby, shit!" Elijah was overwhelmed with pleasure by the way Tasha was deep throating his steel rod. Tasha had dick in her esophagus, and she had Elijah's toes curled.

"Huggh, hughh! You like that baby?" Tasha said as she caught her breath.

"Yeah baby! I like that!" Elijah was loving the oral treatment he was receiving. Let's see how you like this, thought Tasha as she raised Elijah's nutsack and started licking beneath it.

"Ooo oh shit Tasha bae!" Elijah tried to run from Tasha's tongue, but the headboard made him surrender and it gave Tasha the opportunity to lift his leg to go where no one had ever gone before on Elijah. Tasha licked Elijah's asshole making him tense up his body and clutch his ass cheeks at the same time. What the fuck is she trying to do to me? Is this even legal? Elijah questioned himself while he squinched up his face. After thirty seconds of being tensed up Elijah relaxed his body and let Tasha have her way with him. I never thought this would feel so good, thought Elijah as he laid on his back with his legs cocked up while Tasha ate at his salad bar. Eating Elijah's ass had Tasha's pussy pouring honey from it. Tossing salad always turned Tasha on to a different level of freakiness. Now she wanted to feel Elijah inside of her. She wiped her wet face on the bed sheets then she crawled up on Elijah's midsection and inserted his precumming hard dick inside of her dairy delight.

"Ohhh Elijaaaah baaaby! Yoouuu feel sssooooo good!" Cried Tasha as she eased down on Elijah's dick. Elijah reached up and pulled Tasha's face down to his, kissing her feverishly.

"Why you doin me like this? Elijah asked between kisses. He was already whooped. He didn't know if it was his wet ass or Tasha's wet pussy, but he had never felt so good from having sex. I got his ass now, thought Tasha as she tightened her vagina muscles on Elijah's shaft and slowly rode him.

Sinful Behavior

"You the one doing me like this!" Tasha whispered into Elijah's ear sending him overboard.

"Tasha, bae! Chhhmm ehhhmm!" Elijah moaned as he spilled semen inside of Tasha. She gripped his dick even tighter with her pussy, milking his dick until it went soft. Elijah was weak as a crippled man's legs. Tasha gazed into Elijah's eyes.

"I love you!"

"I love you too!" He replied.

"Night night!" Tasha saw that Elijah was bout to fall asleep from the nut he'd just bust. By the time she got off of him to get a soapy rag to clean him up with and came back to the bed to wash him up, Elijah was sleep. "The voodoo is in the Doodoo!" Tasha whispered in Elijah's ears as he slept like a newborn baby that was fall from a bottle of warm milk.

****

Elijah opened his eyes at 6:41 AM to find himself in the bed alone. Where is Tasha? Was his first thought as he sat up in the bed. He searched the bed for his boxers, but when he cut the lamp on, he saw that all of his clothes were neatly folded and placed in the chair next to the desk beside the T.V. Elijah grabbed his phone and called Tasha, but her phone went straight to the voicemail. He noticed that all her belongings were gone. His mind instantly began running wild as of why Tasha left the hotel without even trying to wake him up. Not for one moment did Elijah think about the fact that he'd been out all night as he tried to call Tasha's phone again, but still he got the voicemail. His only concern was locating Tasha, therefore he got dressed and left the hotel. Elijah drove to Tasha's mama's house, but her car wasn't there. That didn't stop Elijah from ringing Coretta's doorbell at 7:30 in the morning.

"Who is it?" Coretta screamed from inside the house.

"It's Pastor Woods!" Elijah answered and the door came open.

"Come in Elijah!" Coretta held a cup of coffee in her hand, dressed in her robe with house shoes on her feet.

"I'm sorry to disturb you, but Tasha and I stayed at the hotel last night, but when I woke up, she was gone!" Ooh! My baby done hooked tha Pastor, thought Coretta as she looked at the worried expression that covered Elijah's face. Coretta wanted to smile, but she had to hide her feelings.

Sinful Behavior

"Oh, my Elijah! I don't know! I haven't heard from her. All I know is for the past few days you have been the only thing that my baby has talked about, but I do know that she has a real fear that you don't really want her!" Coretta knew what her baby was doing, and she was gonna assist Tasha in any way possible.

"Mama Caine, Tasha has my undivided attention. I don't want nothing or nobody else!" Elijah pleaded. My baby got the Pastor in distraught, thought Coretta as she fought to keep a concerned expression on her face.

"I know Elijah, but you gotta look at things from Tasha's view. I don't know what all you know about her life, but that girl has really been hurt! Then her ass broke cause she borrowed the money from me to rent that expensive room y'all stayed in last night!" Coretta was with all the bullshit and games. Elijah looked confused.

"Why didn't she just ask me for the money?"

"She doesn't want you to know about her financial situation and don't tell her that I said anything to you about I loaned her some money for a room!" Coretta watched as Elijah pulled out his wallet from his back pocket and pulled ten blue hundred-dollar bills from inside it.

"Here mama! If she comes over or calls could you tell her to please call me so we can work this out!" Elijah handed Coretta the money.

"Thanks son! I will be sure to tell her as soon as I talk to her!" Elijah kissed Coretta on her cheek then he left. Coretta couldn't get to her phone fast enough after she closed her door behind Elijah. She grabbed her phone and called Tasha, who picked up on the first ring.

"Ma, what's up?"

"Girl! Elijah just left from over here looking like you licked his ass then left him on Mars!" Coretta was full of it.

"For real girl!"

"Yes, hunnie child! You got the Pastor fucked up in the head. Just keep him on blocklist til Sunday then show up at church!" Coretta had all the game.

"Okay ma! You know I'ma do what my OG tell me to do!"

"Good! I told him you borrowed the money from me for that room y'all stayed in last night and he gave me a thousand dollars!" Coretta confessed.

"I'm on my way to get my half!" Tasha wanted her cut.

"Bitch you dead!" Said Coretta then she hung up the phone on Tasha.

"Ma! Ma!" Tasha looked at her phone and seen that Coretta had hung up on her.

Elijah called Tasha's phone more than twenty times from the time he left Coretta's house until he made it home. When the garage door went up Elijah was glad to see that Cynthia's car was gone.

"Door open!" Chimed the ADT Alarm System causing Samantha to quickly throw the comforter next to her over her nude body while Daniel, her friend quickly put on his shirt and pulled up his shorts.

"Samantha what are you doing here? And who is he and why is he here?" Elijah asked when he walked into the den area.

"I'm sick that's why I'm at home! Me and Daniel got a science project to work on that's due tomorrow so he came over so we could work on it!" Samantha spoke with a raspy voice, trying to sound sick.

"Awl! Okay!" Was all Elijah said then he went upstairs to his room.

"Holy shit! Your dad actually bought that bullshit you just sold him!" Daniel couldn't believe what had just happened.

"Shut up and give me that dick!" Samantha reached into Daniel's shorts. Ever since Josh had broken her virginity in the bathroom of the movies, Samantha had to have the feeling she'd experienced every day and she felt that there was no reason to do it with the same guy twice.

Elijah went to his bedroom then he went got in the shower. When he got out of the shower, he wrapped himself around the waist with a towel. Then he went and sat on the edge of his bed and called Tasha's phone. After reaching her voicemail five times, Elijah threw his phone against the wall.

"Fuck!" Elijah screamed out of frustration of not being able to get in touch wit Tasha. He got dressed to leave the house. When he walked downstairs to the den Samantha and Daniel appeared to be working on a school project, so Elijah didn't think nothing of it. Twenty-five minutes later Elijah found himself sitting in his office trying to calculate some business, but he couldn't think of nothing but Tasha, so he gave up on the work and pulled out a bottle of White Hennessy.

****

"Nooo! Bitch you didn't do it to him!" Leikei had not been to sleep in two days because of the Molly she had taken, and Tasha could tell by the way she was moving around.

"Yessss Bitch! I put that nigga in the buck and licked that ass! Bitch sit yo high ass down somewhere!" Tasha couldn't stand the way Leikei kept moving around fidgeting.

"Bitch I can't! That Molly Ralphy gave me got me high as hell! The Slime Gang niggas threw at least a hundred thousand last night!" Leikei pulled out her money to show Tasha what she had made. Tasha felt jealous of Leikei for a minute as she watched her count her money. But then Tasha thought about the fact that she has a millionaire sprung on her. Patience is the virtue, thought Tasha then she helped Leikei count her money.

****

Karter sold a new Aston Martin to a married couple for $150,000. He had made ten grand off the sale and it wasn't 11 o'clock yet. Today is a great day, thought Karter as he got up from his desk to walk outside to the lot. When he reached the lot from a distance, he seen a woman in a scrub outfit bent overlooking inside one of the cars. Karter didn't see anyone assisting her so he thought he should help the woman who had just took a seat inside of the Bentley Coupe she was looking at. Karter straightened his tie and cleared his throat as he made his approach, while the woman leaned over into the car next to the Bently Coupe.

"Hi ma'am! Can I help you today?" Karter couldn't see the woman's face from where he was standing, but he couldn't help but notice how her thighs were filling up the scrubs she was wearing.

"Yes, you can handsome!" Cynthia stepped out of the car smiling catching Karter by surprise.

"Wow! Cynthia! What a surprise!" Karter was shocked to see Cynthia at his job.

"You've been on my mind and I wanted to look at a few cars for Samantha!" Cynthia closed in on Karter, got on her tippy toes and then she kissed him. Karter reacted by hugging her.

"Damn you soft Cynt!" Karter said into Cynthia's ear.

"And wet too!" Cynthia proclaimed. Karter had a special effect on her. He stepped back to look at Cynthia.

"Are we still on for tomorrow?" Karter had been anticipating the masquerade.

"Of course, we are! Walk me to my car!" Karter followed behind Cynthia while she walked to her car. He watched Cynthia's big junky booty jiggle as she walked. Cynthia was dumb, thick, fine and a honey bun away from being fat. I know for a fact that is too much ass for my lil dick, thought Karter as he imagined himself trying to fuck Cynthia from the back. Cynthia opened the driver's side door to her car then she leaned inside to get a bag off the passenger seat. When she bent over a portion of her ass crack and panties got exposed. Karter couldn't stop himself from what he was about to do. She's a freak anyways, thought Karter as he quickly scoped the scene to make sure the coast was clear. Then he stuck his hand into Cynthia's pants.

"Ehhmmm!" Cynthia bent over more to give him more access to dig deeper, which he did until he felt her juices on his fingers. Karter quickly snatched his hand out of Cynthia's pants, and she raised up out of the car.

"Don't start nothing that you can't finish!" Cynthia grabbed Karter's hand and guided it to his nose. The lovely smell of clean ass and wet pussy invaded Karter's nostrils releasing the dopamine in his brain, getting him high off of her scent. Cynthia smiled at the expression on Karter's face.

"Woman you gonna get me fired!" They both laughed

"Here crazy, I bought us both something to wear tomorrow. I hope you like yours and here's your ticket to the masquerade." Cynthia handed Karter a gift bag from Pleasures. He looked into the bag. There was a pair of boxers and a mask inside of it.

"Yes, baby I like it!"

"Well give me a kiss so I can leave!" Karter wrapped his arms around Cynthia's waist and kissed her. Cynthia broke their kiss.

"You've gotten me wet as fuck! I gotta go before I take that dick!" Cynthia didn't give Karter a chance to speak. She jumped into her car and pulled off. He put his

Sinful Behavior

hand to his nose while he walked to his car to put up the gift bag. Cynthia's scent made his dick get hard instantly. Cynthia had him so turned on that he sat inside of his car and did something that he hadn't never did before. Karter unzipped his pants and pulled out his Jimmie.

"Here goes nothin Lil Buddy!" Karter snapped a picture of his dick with his phone and sent the picture to Cynthia.

"I can't believe we just did that Lil Buddy!" Karter told his lil man as he tucked him away.

Cynthia opened the message from Karter while she waited in the drive-thru at Starbucks. A smile the size of the moon spread across her face when she saw the picture of Karter's four-inch hard dick. Umm, look at that lil pretty dick, thought Cynthia as she felt her mouth water and her pussy moisten. She had only felt one dick inside of her in her entire life besides her toy, but she knew she was for sure looking at number two. Cynthia had always wanted to try what she had seen Dr. Feel Good and other porn stars do in their videos. Looking at the size of Karter's dick she knew that she had found the perfect partner to fulfill her fantasy. Cynthia quickly texted Karter back.

Sent- (To KJ)- I can't wait to meet him handsome. I want you to put him where no man has ever gone before.

Karter was in shock when he read Cynthia's message. Damn she wants me to fuck her in the ass, thought Karter as he read Cynthia's message for the fifth time before he finally replied.

Sent – (To Cynt) – Baby you can do whatever makes you happy! I'll see you tomorrow.

Sinful Behavior

CHAPTER 5

Elijah started his Saturday morning just like he ended his Friday night, calling Tasha's phone. He was so far gone over Tasha that he didn't care that he was in the bed next to Cynthia while he called Tasha's phone.

"You have reached the voicemail of 404-!" Elijah listened to Tasha's voicemail one last time before he got out of the bed. His mind was on nothing but Tasha even though he had a basketball game at 11 o'clock.

Elijah felt sluggish so he tried taking a shower to get himself going, but his mind wouldn't allow him to think pass Tasha. When he got out of the shower, he heard his phone ringing in the bedroom. Elijah literally ran in the bedroom wet, dripping water from his body. He picked up his phone, seen that it was a church member and didn't even answer it. He threw the phone back onto the bed and walked back to the bathroom to get his towel. That girl has really got my husband gone over her, thought Cynthia while she laid in the bed waiting for Elijah to leave out of the room so she could text Karter.

"What do you got up for the day hubby?" Cynthia asked Elijah when he walked into the bedroom looking like someone had stolen his dog.

"I got a game at eleven. Then I gotta prepare for tomorrow's service so I'll be at the church all night!" Elijah's tone was dry as sand.

"Do you wanna spend some time with me and the kids tonight? We can go to the movies, bowling or something!" Cynthia already knew his answer as she stretched her arms in the air.

"No! I don't have time, but y'all need to be in service on time in the morning!" Elijah hadn't looked at Cynthia one time while he talked to her. He threw on a t-shirt some gym shorts and Jordan sneakers then he departed the bedroom. Cynthia laughed. He really has some nerve, thought Cynthia while she texted Karter, good morning.

"Dad can we talk for a minute?" Elijah Jr. asked his dad. He wanted to tell his dad about his sexuality in front of his lover Jason, who was sitting next to him on the couch.

"Not right now! I don't have time. Make sure that you're at church tomorrow on time!" Elijah didn't even

Sinful Behavior

look at his son. He just walked right past Jr. and went into the garage to leave. Jr. laid his head into Jason's lap and started crying. He was emotionally torn. He needed to talk to his father, but it seemed as if his father didn't care.

"It's gonna be okay baby! I love you!" Jason ran his fingers through Jr.'s hair. Jr. wiped his tears and looked up at Jason.

"Do you really love me?" Jr. knew that he loved Jason.

"Yes, I love you!" Jason said in his baritone voice. Jr. pulled Jason's dick out from his gym shorts and stuck it in his mouth. Jason smiled as he laid his head back on the couch, he loved Jr.'s head game.

Elijah called Tasha's phone the entire drive to church. He was stressed out that he hadn't talked to Tasha. He didn't even know that he hadn't eaten in two days. When he seen that Tasha had him blocked on social media, he got even sicker. It was as if Tasha had Elijah under some type of spell. For two days he had been leaving voicemails on Tasha's phone telling her how much he loved her and missed her. Elijah even went back to Mother Caine's house last night to try to catch Tasha over there, but Coretta told him that she hadn't seen Tasha.

Michael "Oodoo" Smith

When Elijah pulled up at church the parking lot was almost full since there was three games with the first one being played at 9 AM. He looked at the dashboard and saw that it was 10 o'clock. I have an hour to try to prepare a sermon for tomorrow, thought Elijah as he got out of the car dragging like he had no energy.

"Hi Pastor!"

"Good morning Pastor!"

"Good luck on your game Pastor!" Members of the church spoke to Elijah on his way inside the church, Elijah threw his hand up and kept walking.

Karter pulled into the church parking lot feeling good. He was ready to get his ball on. But even more so he was ready for the night to get there so he could meet Cynthia at the Masquerade.

"Hey Deacon Jones!" Brother James spoke to Karter. "Hi Brother James! How are y'all doing? Look at lil George, he's getting huge!" Karter put a big smile on James's face. He shook their hands then he went into the church. He seen Elijah's car, so he figured he was inside.

"Baby he's more polite then Pastor Woods!" Said Sister James.

Sinful Behavior

"You're right baby! I noticed that too!" Brother James agreed with his wife.

"Who is it?" Elijah screamed when someone knocked on his office door.

"It's Deacon Jones!" Elijah opened the door then he went flopped down on the couch. Karter looked at Elijah's body language and he knew something was seriously wrong with him. Karter walked in the office and shut the door behind him.

"What's up bruh? Where you been? Ain heard from you!" Karter sat on the edge of Elijah's desk.

"I've been around! Just ain't been feelin like being bothered!" Elijah was dry as he stared up at the ceiling.

"Do you wanna talk about it?" Karter offered. Elijah quickly sat up straight on the couch and looked Karter in the eyes.

"I love Tasha and I won't be able to get right until I have her as my woman. I haven't talked to her since she left me at the hotel the other night after she put me to bed and it's killing me!" Elijah confessed. Karter couldn't believe the words that had come out of Elijah's mouth.

"Damn bruh! What about Cynthia?"

"I can't even look at her! She disgust me!" Elijah admitted. Damn, this dude is really tripped out, thought Karter as he stood up from the desk.

"Well I hope you get it together, cause you don't look like yourself! I'm finna go to the gym and get ready for the game!" Karter walked to the door to leave.

"Karter, I need to ask you something!"

"Yeah bruh! What's up?" Please don't say Cynthia's name, thought Karter as he grew nervous to what Elijah was about to ask him.

"Have you ever had your ass licked?"

"Huh?" Karter was confused.

"What do you mean, like has a woman ever licked my butt?" Karter had wrinkles in his forehead,

"No! Has a woman ever licked your ass hole?" Elijah explained in plain and simple English. Karter was shocked.

"Nawl bruh! That ain't ever happened to me! Hell, I've never even had anal sex with a chick before!"

Sinful Behavior

"Bruh, listen to me! Don't ever let a woman lick your asshole! I think the Voodoo is in the Doodoo!" Karter laughed at Elijah's statement.

"You laughin but I'm dead serious!" Elijah was dead serious.

"Ha! I'm gone bruh!" Wow! This nigga has tripped the fuck out, thought Karter as he ran out of the office.

Forty minutes later the game started, and Elijah was just on the court. He wasn't into the game at all. It was clear to the players and the people in the stands that Elijah's mind was somewhere else. Brotha Davis killed Elijah the whole game. He even dunked on Elijah in the third quarter. If it wasn't for Karter scoring a triple double and hitting the game winning three pointer with one second on the clock, their team would've lost.

The crowd went crazy when Karter hit the buzzer beater and they ran onto the court to congratulate Karter on the shot. The two teams shook hands, but Elijah didn't attend. He walked off the court with his head down and only one thing on his mind, Tasha. After the game several members of the church asked Karter was Elijah alright and Karter assured them that the pastor was okay. Some of the church members even told Karter that he should consider being pastor. Karter laughed it off and told them that he might consider it one day. Karter's phone vibrated as he exited the gym. It was a video message from Thomas. Karter pressed play.

"3, 2, 1, swishhh!" Yelled the crowd on the video of Karter hitting the game winning shot. Karter smiled from ear to ear as he watched the captivating moment. When he looked up from his phone Thomas was walking in his direction.

"What's up bruh? Thanks for the video!" Karter told Thomas as they gave each other daps and hugs. Then Thomas texted Karter.

Rcvd from Brother Thomas – Good game! Ya homie didn't look to good tho!

"I know right!" Karter replied.

"I'll get up with you later! I got a few things to do before my date tonight!" Karter told Thomas who started texting.

"Tell Cynthia I said hi!" Thomas held his stomach while he silently laughed when Karter read the message. How does he know about Cynthia, Karter asked himself.

Sinful Behavior

"I'll do that!" Karter dapped up Thomas then he got in his car and left.

****

Cynthia looked at herself in the full-length body mirror to make sure that she was satisfied with her appearance. Her long hair flowed past her shoulders and her breast sat up in the black lace negligee she was wearing. Cynthia's ass and thick thighs were bodacious. Her caramel skin was glowing. She went earlier in the day and got a pedicure and manicure so everything about her appearance was on point. The Kim Wooo heels she had on made her four inches taller. Cynthia threw on a thin black trench coat and left out of her room. When she made it to the den area Samantha was on the couch asleep. Cynthia didn't bother to wake her up, she just left. As soon as Samantha heard Cynthia's car crank and the garage door go up, she grabbed her phone.

"Yeah!" T-Fat answered his phone. Samantha had met him earlier in the day when she was with her friends at the Lenoxx Mall.

"Hey! What's up?" Samantha tried to sound older than what she was. When she met T-Fat she told him that she was twenty years old.

"Who dis?" T-Fat asked as he pulled off the blunt of Sugar Breath that he was smokin.

"Samantha!"

"Aw, what's up shawty!"

"You!"

"Oh yeah! You trying to get out wit me?" He asked her.

"That was my plans for tonight!" Samantha said sarcastically.

"Yeah shawty! Text me the address and I'm on my way!" T-Fat wanted to get out the "Trap" For a minute anyways.

"Okay Daddy! I'm waiting!" Samantha hung up the phone, texted T-Fat her address then she ran up to her room to put on the skimpiest outfit she could find and apply as much make-up to her face that it would hold.

Cynthia called Karter's phone as she turned into the parking lot of the Intercontinental Hotel.

"What's up beautiful?" Karter turned on his exit.

Sinful Behavior

"You, handsome! Where you at?" Cynthia pulled to the front of the hotel for valet Parking.

"I'm about to turn in! Where you at?"

"I'm in line for valet parking!" Cynthia noticed that the valet attendant was handing the people in the cars in front of her an envelope and the cars were pulling off.

"For some reason nobody is getting out their car. Unless they come for another event!" Cynthia was confused.

"Just see what's goin on! I'm getting in the line now!" Karter pulled into the line of cars.

"Ok! Hold on!" Cynthia rolled down her window.

"Hi ma'am! Are you here for the Masquerade?" The valet asked Cynthia.

"Yes, I am!"

"Can I have your ticket?" Cynthia opened her Hermes clutch purse and got her ticket out.

"Here you go!" Cynthia handed valet her ticket.

"Here you are ma'am! Just follow the instructions on the invitation inside the envelope. You must have that to get in!"

'Thanks! Karter!" Cynthia pulled off.

"Yeah, I'm here!" Karter pulled forward in the line.

"The valet is gonna give you an invitation when you give him your ticket. Do you wanna ride with me or you scared?" Cynthia joked.

"Ha! Ha! Real funny! Park over there by the water fountain while I get this invitation!" After Karter got his invitation, he pulled up next to Cynthia in the hotel parking lot. Cynthia felt moisture between her thighs when Karter hopped out his car holding his mask, wearing nothing but some silk boxers and Gucci house shoes, which was the gift that Cynthia had bought for him to wear.

"Damn Mr. Jones! Why don't we just get a room?" Cynthia's mouth watered as she looked at Karter's smooth brown skin glisten under the moonlight.

"Nope! You wanna see this Dr. Feel Good muthafucka, so that's where we're going!" Said Karter as he leaned onto Cynthia's door.

Sinful Behavior

"Okay! Well, who's gonna drive?" She asked.

"I'm ridin with you, beautiful!" Karter walked around to the passenger side and got out into the front seat.

****

"Damn lil baby! Y'all living good thang ah muthafucka, ain't ya!" B-Fat was trippin on how big Samantha's house was.

"I guess that means your outside!" Samantha grabbed her purse and headed for the front door almost trippin in her mama's Red Bottoms that were too big for her, plus she was an amateur heel walker. She walked outside and got in the Ocean Blue Tahoe that squatted on 34-inch Forged Asanti's. Since there was a dude sitting in the front seat. Samantha opened the back door and got in.

"Got damn! Lil Shawty slim thick ain't it mane!" Said D-Fat who was sitting next to Samantha in the back. B-Fat and J-Fat turned around to get a good look at Samantha. She quickly noticed that none of them was the dude she met at the mall.

"Hell yeah! Lil shawty ass ready!" J-Fat was drooling from the mouth.

"Where is T-Fat?" Samantha asked curious about what was going on.

"We were closer to you than he was, so he gave us the address to swing through and pick you up!" B-Fat told Samantha as he reversed out of the driveway.

"Oh, so you taking me to him?"

"Yeah Lil shawty! You smoke?"

"Yeah!" Samantha lied. D-Fat hit the blunt of Girl Scout Cookies then passed it to Samantha and she tried to hit the blunt like she was a veteran.

Cugh Cugh Cugh

"That's that pressure lil shawty!" Said D-Fat and Samantha handed him the blunt back. Then she wiped the tear from her eye. I bet this lil hoe is a "Go-Live-er", thought D-Fat then he reached over and rubbed Samantha's thigh. She looked at D-Fat, who flashed his gold grill, smiling.

He's cute, thought Samantha. Then she put her hand on top of his hand and guided his hand up her thigh and under the skirt she was wearing. Oh shit, thought D-Fat as he unbuckled his Balmain jeans, pulled out his dick and put Samantha's hand on it. Samantha smiled at D-Fat then she leaned over and did what she had been watching Montana Fishburne do to Dr. Feel Good on the porn she was watching on her phone.

Slurp Slurp Slurp

J-Fat and B-Fat were talking to one another until they heard slurping. They turned around to see what was going on. D-Fat hit the interior light above his head to give them a better view. J-Fat climbed in the back of the truck to join the action.

****

After listening to Cynthia pour out her heart for the last twenty minutes, Karter understood why she was a different person from the girl he grew up knowing. Karter couldn't believe that out of the past eight years Elijah and Cynthia had been intimate less than fifty times. The more Cynthia compared Elijah to her father, the more things made sense to him. Karter knew Elijah was gonna faint when he found out that his son was gay, but like Cynthia said, he's so caught up on Tasha that he doesn't care about anything else.

"Turn that up, sexy!" Karter had his mind made up and he didn't wanna hear anything else about Elijah.

Music: I know you wanna be

In my B-E-D

Grinding slowly

Karter sang along with Jacquees as he reached over and caressed Cynthia's thigh while she drove.

"Karter, stop! I can't drive with you touching me!" Cynthia felt electrical currents run through her body when Karter touched her. Karter took his hand from her leg, but he leaned over, undid the button to open her coat, and he pulled her breast out of the negligee she was wearing.

"Okay, I'll stop!" Said Karter then he began sucking on her nipple.

"Siii! Kaaaaaaarter!" Cynthia moaned as she tried to focus on the road. Karter took one last nibble on her nipple.

"Okay, I quit!" Karter put Cynthia's breast back inside of her negligee.

"Destination 50 feet to the left!" The navigation system sounded through the car speakers. When Karter and

Sinful Behavior

Cynthia looked to their left, they saw one of the biggest houses either one of them had ever seen. The 10,000 square feet house was beyond extraordinary. They pulled in the line at the gate, which closed once a single car went through.

"What do I do now?" Cynthia asked when she pulled up in front of the gate.

"On the invitation it says to punch in the word LOVE on the security keypad!" Cynthia rolled her window down and punched in the code and the iron gate came open for her to drive through. They moved forward slowly in the line. When they made it to the front of the house there was a black man of medium build wearing only a bowtie and a pair of house shoes on the passenger side of the car. On the driver's side stood a naked Spanish woman who only had on heels.

"Now that's what's up!" Cynthia liked the scenery already.

"I bet it is!" Karter said as he turned his head from looking at the man standing at his door with a baby leg sitting between his legs.

"Please let me see your invitation!" The lady instructed Cynthia, who handed her both invitations.

"Your car number is 300! Please walk to the front door!" The black man walked around to Cynthia's door and opened the car door for her. Karter got out on his own. Damn Cynthia's ass is super fat, thought Karter as he watched Cynthia's ass jiggle on their walk to the front door of the mansion. He noticed a clear substance running down her inner thigh. Cynthia hadn't been able to stop her pussy from pulsating since Karter sucked on her tittie. When they reached the door, Cynthia rang the doorbell. The door came open and there stood a man and a woman almost identical to the man and woman that had told them to go to the house. Cynthia and Karter couldn't believe their eyes. The entire mansion seemed to be filled with naked men and women of all ages, sizes and nationalities.

"You can come with us or you can free-lance as a couple!" The naked black man told them. Cynthia couldn't help but to stare at his luscious dick.

"We're gonna free-lance as a couple!" Karter answered. The man pulled a clear clothing bag from off the table next to where they were standing.

Sinful Behavior

"That's fine! Please place all of your clothing in this bag including your shoes!" Cynthia wasted no time taking off her negligee and heels, but Karter was hesitant. Fuck, I thought she said I could wear my boxers, thought Karter then he took off his clothes. Cynthia seen how uncomfortable he was.

"Baby you don't have nothing to be ashamed of, look!" Cynthia pointed to a man who's dick damn near wasn't visible by the human eye. Karter laughed.

"I guess you're right!" He quickly shook off his insecurity.

"Your bag will be in the cubby 517!" Said the beautiful Spanish lady then her and the black man disappeared into the house. A waitress appeared handing Cynthia and Karter a glass of champagne.

"Well, I guess we should tour the house!" Karter suggested.

"Let's do it!" Cynthia didn't want the man walking towards her with his dick swinging past his kneecaps to think that she was alone and try to approach her, so she locked her arm into Karter's arm. But that didn't stop the 6-foot 7-inch man with salt and pepper hair from approaching her. That can't be real, thought Cynthia when the gorilla looking black man got within arm's reach of her.

"Hi bootifuul! Ya have de most bootifulist skin me has eva seen!" The man's accent let Karter and Cynthia both know he was from the Islands somewhere.

"Thank you!" Cynthia looked up at Karter.

"Hell, go ahead and touch it baby!" Karter read Cynthia's mind.

"Can I touch, you know?" Cynthia shyly asked the man.

"Shuur! Go head! Me wish me was smalla like he so I could get rock harda!" The man made a fist with one hand and pointed at Karter's dick with the other. Cynthia reached out and grabbed the man's dick by the head.

"Oh my god! This thing has to weigh at least ten pounds." Cynthia was amazed at how heavy the man's dick was.

"Eleven pounds, 3 ouncez to be exact!" Said the man smiling. Cynthia and Karter burst into laughter. Cynthia let go of the man's elephant trunk and as soon as she did two young white girls that were around the age of twenty-three came and fell to their knees. The two girls sucked away at the man's huge dick like it was the God of Dicks.

"See baby he said that he wished that he was your size so that he could get hard!" Cynthia got on her tippy toes and kissed Karter.

"Yeah, I'm glad me and my lil buddy don't have that problem!" Karter handed Cynthia a wet wipe after they kissed to wipe her hands off.

They walked deeper into the house and discovered groups of people having orgies. One woman even reached out and grabbed Karter's dick while she got fucked. Cynthia smiled while she watched the woman give Karter a quick hand jig. Next, they walked up the spiraling staircase of the house that led to the bedrooms with "Enter at your own risk" signs hanging on the doorknobs. Karter and Cynthia looked at one another after they read the sign.

"Open it up, scary cat!" Karter told Cynthia. She opened the door and peeped inside. Wow thought Cynthia when she saw everyone inside with glowing dicks, tits and pussies. She stepped into the room and pulled Karter inside, then closed the door. Karter smirked at all of the glowing going on. A petite Asian woman walked up to

Karter then fell to her knees. She put a glow condom in her mouth and then put Karter's dick between her lips. When she took her mouth off of Karter's dick, it was glowing like all the rest of the dicks in the room. The Asian woman stood up from her knees and held out her hand. Cynthia and Karter looked at the contents in her hand, which appeared to be some type of capsules.

"Molly!" Said the Asian woman.

"No thanks! We're good!" Cynthia quickly told the woman.

"Attention ladies and gentlemen! Dr. Feel Good is in the living room right now, getting ready to do a live performance." Said a voice on the surround sound system.

"Come on baby! Let's go!" Cynthia was ready to get the hell away from the Molly Glow Gang, therefore her and Karter left out of the room and went downstairs to the living room. To their surprise there was only around 15 people in the huge living room standing in front of a California King size bed attending the live show.

"Look bay! That's him!" Cynthia told Karter when Dr. Feel Good walked into the room. Dr. Feel Good stood 6 feet 1 inch, wore a bald head, had light brown skin and

Sinful Behavior

had the typical medium built body. But he had no tattoos and a ten-inch dick that he knew how to work like a nuclear weapon. He gained the undivided attention of everyone when he walked into the room naked, shaking hands with people in attendance of the show. One lady fainted when he shook her hand.

"You have such beautiful skin!" Dr. Feel Good told Cynthia as he looked into her eyes while he shook her hand. Cynthia's pussy spurted out a mist of cum. She had fucked herself to so many of his videos now she was actually naked holding Dr. Feel Good's hand.

"Thank you handsome!" Cynthia replied. Then Dr. Feel Good greeted the rest of the crowd while a gorgeous naked Brazilian woman climbed into the large bed.

"Hi! I'm glad you all made it out! I can see that everyone is enjoying themselves considering the fact that there's less than twenty people attending the live show!" Everyone laughed at his statement because he was telling the truth. There was over 250 people in the house, but less than ten percent of them showed up to the main event. He continued.

"Y'all know what! Tonight, we're gonna do something new! Who in here can tell me the name of my first porn video?" Dr. Feel Good asked the crowd. Cynthia unconsciously raised her hand. He pointed at her.

"The woman with the most beautifulest skin that I've ever seen! Give it to me!"

"Thick Chicks Fucking Big Dicks!" Cynthia was positive of her answer.

"You are correct! Come here!" Dr Feel Good waved for Cynthia to come stand next to him. She looked at Karter.

"Gone up there baby!" Karter was happy for Cynthia. She walked up to the front and stood next to Dr. Feel Good.

"So, you are a true fan, huh?" Dr. Feel Good looked at Cynthia with pure seduction in his eyes.

"I am!" Cynthia smiled.

"That's good to know! Who's here with you?"

"My friend Karter!" Cynthia pointed to Karter.

"Come on up here, Karter!" Dr. Feel Good waved for Karter to come up front. Fuck thought Karter. He didn't want to be in the spotlight. Cynthia leaned over and whispered something to Dr. Feel Good causing him to shake his head. Dr. Feel Good walked up to Karter and grabbed him by the arm. He led Karter up to the front next to Cynthia.

"We don't do the shy thing in here! I don't know what you shy about. That's your dick! Love your dick no matter what size it is. Love him for who he is!" Dr. Feel Good had just caused Karter to get over his insecurities forever.

"I'm gonna get you!" Karter told Cynthia while he laughed.

"You are right, my brother! You are gonna get her. As a matter of fact, we are gonna get her together. Excuse me Miss Lady, but could you get out of the bed for us. The Brazilian woman reluctantly got out of the bed.

"So, Misses Pretty Skin! If you could have Dr. Feel Good and Karter at the same damn time like you've seen so many times in my videos, what would you like for us to do to you?" Dr Feel Good asked Cynthia who was smiling from ear to ear.

"I wanna suck your dick while Karter fucks me from the back!" Cynthia knew exactly what she wanted.

"Tonight, is your night beautiful!" Dr Feel Good grabbed Cynthia by her hand and guided her body into the center of the bed. Then he positioned her on all fours.

"Karter! Get in the bed and get behind her!" Karter did as he was told. When he got behind Cynthia she turned around and pulled off the glow in the dark condom he had on. Then she turned back around and assumed the position. Dr. Feel Good stood at the side of the bed in front of Cynthia. The way everybody's body was positioned it was like the crowd was watching a porn. Dr. Feel Good handed Cynthia a condom.

"Put that on my dick and make Dr. Feel Good feel good! Karter, what you waiting on? Fuck that pussy!" Cynthia and Karter went to work doing what the Dr. had ordered. This was the first time that Cynthia and Karter were having sex and they were doing it with a pornstar in front of a crowd of people.

"Oooooh Karter!" Cynthia moaned when Karter slid the head of his thick four-inch dick inside of her extremely wet pussy as she rolled the condom onto Dr. Feel Good's dick. Her wetness drenched Karter's dick as she put the head of Dr. Feel Good's dick in her mouth. The activity Cynthia was engaged in had her boiling on the insides.

"Fuck me harder!" Cynthia demanded while she stroked the shaft of Dr. Feel Good's big dick. Karter grabbed her by her hips and started giving her everything he had. There was something about the short hard jabs that Karter was delivering to Cynthia's pussy that sent her into ecstasy. She let go of Dr. Feel Good's dick and laid her face down on the bed with her ass in the air at a 90-degree angle, which gave Karter a direct stroke to her G-Spot.

"Oooh, ooh yessss!" Cynthia screamed while she clawed the bed sheets. Dr. Feel Good couldn't believe his eyes as he watched Cynthia's pussy spurt cum onto Karter's midsection while he fucked her from the back. Dr. feel Good pointed to his assistant for her to start recording. Karter was experiencing the best pussy he'd ever had.

"Kaaaaarter babbbyyy rigggght there!" Cynthia's pussy kept skeeting cum onto Karter's abs as he pumped hard, making sure that his balls slapped against Cynthia's clitoris with every pump he took. Cynthia used her vagina muscles to grab ahold of Karter's dick and he immediately felt his nut comin.

Michael "Oodoo" Smith

"Ugghhhhm, ugghmmm! Ahh shit! Cyynt!" Was all Karter managed to say before he locked his ass cheeks, to one last stroke and stuffed everything he had into Cynthia spilling his semen inside of her. The feeling of Karter's hot load shooting into her sent Cynthia into an orgasm.

"Kaaaaarter baaaaay!" Cynthia's body started shaking as she collapsed onto the bed no longer able to hold herself up. Karter collapsed on top of her. That was the greatest show on earth thought Dr. Feel Good who started clapping along with the on lookers.

"I love you, Cynt!" Karter said into Cynthia's ear causing her to smile. She turned onto her back while she lay beneath Karter and looked him in the eyes.

"I'm in love with you, Karter!" Cynthia meant every word.

After the sex scene was over Karter and Cynthia were ready to leave. They got dressed in a small room near the front door and right when they were about to exit the mansion, Dr. Feel Good approached them.

"Excuse me Mr. Little Big Man and Miss Pretty Skin!" Cynthia and Karter both laughed.

Sinful Behavior

"Here's my card if either of you ever want a job in the industry, give me a call!" Dr. Feel Good handed them both his contact card then he disappeared back into the mansion. They shook their heads and laughed as they exited the mansion. Cynthia insisted that Karter drove back to the InterContinental where his car was at. He did so and she gave him head the entire ride there causing him to swerve off the road several times.

"Aihhh! Cyyynt!" Karter moaned as he parked next to his car and reclined the seat all the way back so he could comfortably enjoy the head he was receiving. Cynthia slowly took Karter's dick in and out of her mouth. Karter reached over between her ass cheeks and unsnapped the negligee she had on. Then he stuck two fingers inside of her melting pot.

"Yessss deeeeeper!" Cooed Cynthia when she felt Karter's fingers penetrate her boiling hot pussy.

"Ooh yesss!" Cynthia cried as she gripped Karter's nutsack and stroked his dick with her other hand.

"Siii Cynt! Ahhh!" Karter threw his head back in pleasure.

"I'm cummmin Daaaaddyyyy! Emmmmm!" Cynthia took all of Karter's dick into her mouth as she came all over his hand. The vibration she made with her mouth on his dick sent Karter overboard.

"Cyynt, baa, I, ashhhh!" Karter released in Cynthia's mouth dropping a load of nut so heavy that it almost knocked a hole in the back of her throat, but Cynthia didn't stop. She kept pulling on the head of Karter's dick with her lips causing his body to jerk from the pleasurable pain he was enduring by Cynthia suckin on his tender dick.

"Ehhhhmmmm, baaaaby please stop!" Karter cried out like a lil bitch. Cynthia raised her head from his lap and sat down in the passenger seat with a smile on her face.

"I really enjoyed you tonight, Karter!" Cynthia admitted.

"I enjoyed you more than you'll ever know, beautiful!" Karter raised up and looked at Cynthia.

"I don't want to depart from you!" Karter wanted Cynthia to go home with him. Cynthia felt her eyes get watery and emotions kicked in.

Sinful Behavior

"I don't want to be without you Karter!" Cynthia started crying. Karter reached over and took her in his arms.

"You make me happy!" Cried Cynthia.

"You make me happy too baby! Let's make sure this is what we both want and then we'll go from there!" Karter told Cynthia as they broke their embrace.

"You promise?"

"I promise baby!" Karter replied and they began kissing.

"I guess I'll see you tomorrow at church!" Cynthia laughed.

"Haha! So, you gotta come to church tomorrow!" Karter teased.

"Yeah! I hope Tasha's there!" Cynthia said catching Karter off guard.

"Oh yeah! Why is that?" Karter was curious.

"No reason! I just wanna see how everyone acts!" Cynthia got out of the car and walked to the driver's side. Karter got out of the car and they kissed. After their kiss they went their separate ways. Cynthia thought about

Karter on her entire ride home. When she turned into the driveway the clock on the dashboard read 12:37 AM. She was surprised to see that Elijah was at home when the garage door went up. Damn, thought Cynthia as she grabbed the sweat suit off the backseat and threw it on over the negligee she was wearing.

Cynthia walked in the house expecting to see Samantha on the couch asleep, but the den was empty. Cynthia went upstairs to Samantha's room, but she wasn't there neither. Huhmm, I wonder where she at, thought Cynthia as she pulled out her phone and called Samantha, who's phone went directly to the mailbox. Cynthia hung up and called Jr.'s phone as she walked to her bedroom.

"What's up mom?" Jr. answered on the first ring.

"Have you seen your sister?"

"No! I haven't talked to her!"

"Okay! I'll call you back!" Cynthia said as she walked into her bedroom.

"A got damn shame! It's one o'clock in the morning and you don't know where our fifteen-year-old daughter is at!" Elijah shook his head in disgust with

Cynthia as he sat in the bed slick trying to stalk Tasha's social media.

"When I left, she was on the couch asleep!" Cynthia explained.

"A mouth will say anything!" Elijah commented.

Ding Dong Ding Dong

The doorbell to the front door of the house rang. Elijah got up from the bed to look out of his bedroom window to see who was at his front door. What are the police doing here, thought Elijah.

"That's the police at our door. They probably bringing home our daughter or even worse comin to tell us she dead!" Elijah said sarcastically, but Cynthia didn't find his words humorous. She followed Elijah downstairs to the front door and sure enough when he opened the front door, the police were there with Samantha.

"Hi Pastor Woods and Mrs. Woods!" Said Officer Burgess who happened to be a member of Elijah's church.

"Brother Burgess, what did Samantha do?" Elijah was embarrassed.

"She didn't do anything! I was working security at McDonalds in Bankhead when I saw her walk in the restaurant with some known drug dealers who are far much older than her. When I asked her what she was doing with the dudes, she told me that one of them was her boyfriend. I asked the dudes she was with did they know that she was fifteen and they said that she told them that she was twenty. I told them to get away from her right then before I locked them up for statutory rape!" Elijah couldn't believe his ears as he listened to Officer Burgess.

"Get in the house now Samantha!" Elijah yelled at Samantha and she ran into her mother's arms.

"Thank you so much, Brother Burgess! How could I ever repay you?" Elijah shook his head.

"Just doing my job Pastor! Y'all have a good night!" Officer Burgess shook Elijah's hand then left. Elijah shut the door.

"Get your ass upstairs to your room! I'm finna beat your muthafuckin ass!" Elijah tried to snatch Samantha out of Cynthia's arms.

Sinful Behavior

"No mama! Don't let him whoop me!" Samantha screamed as she clutched on to Cynthia. She had never had a whooping before.

"Leave her alone Elijah! You need to talk to her!" Cynthia spoke calmly as she held onto her baby. Elijah looked at Cynthia like she was beyond ignorant.

"Bitch, you talk to her with your dumb ass. Fuck this shit! I got other shit to worry about!" Elijah walked upstairs. Cynthia had never heard Elijah use the language he'd just used on her or their daughter.

More important than your own daughter, thought Cynthia as she led Samantha to the den couch, where they stayed up for two hours talking. Cynthia explained to Samantha why she shouldn't be doing the things that she was doing. After talking to Samantha Cynthia went upstairs to the guest bedroom where she showered, then got in the bed.

"Lord please make a way for me and Karter to be together and for me to get out of this horrible marriage!" Cynthia prayed before she went to sleep.

CHAPTER 6

Music playing:

> The more I seek him
>
> The more I find him
>
> The more I find him
>
> The more I love him

The choir sang in harmony as the church celebrated its Remembrance Program, which was the one Sunday out of the year dedicated to all the Pastors, Deacons, Mothers and any other member of the church that was deceased. Karter couldn't help but to stare at Cynthia as she sat on the front row wearing a beautiful white dress with her neck laced in pearls. My baby so pretty, thought Karter. He has been staring at Cynthia for the past hour. He knew nobody could tell where he was looking due to the Prada shades he was wearing. He couldn't help but to wonder what was going through Cynthia's mind as she sat two people down from Coretta Caine.

Sinful Behavior

Elijah stood up from his seat in the pulpit when the Choir began to end the song they were singing. He was extraordinary clean in the short sleeve teal blue Versace shirt and pants set he was wearing with matching Versace loafers.

"How is everyone doing today? I'm glad to see everyone make it out to our Remembrance Program. Even my lovely wife is present today!"

"Bout time!" Someone in the congregation said and several people started laughing.

"Hmm! I couldn't agree more with you! Mrs. Woods does need to attend service more often!" Cynthia couldn't believe what Elijah was saying. He is the anti-Christ, thought Cynthia as she fought to keep a smile on her face. Coretta Caine leaned forward and looked at Cynthia, then she rolled her eyes. It took everything in Karter's will power for him not to go into the pulpit and commence to beating Elijah's ass. Karter was so mad that sweat formed on his forehead.

"For everyone who doesn't know why our Remembrance Program is so important, today is the day we......" A lump formed in Elijah's throat and it became hard for him to swallow as he watched Tasha walk into the church.

Tasha looked like she fell from heaven as she walked down the aisle wearing a white Alexander McQueen fitted gown dress with four-inch Louis Vuitton heels on her feet. Elijah took a sip of water and unbuttoned the top button of his shirt while he watched Tasha sit directly behind Cynthia. Damn, there goes my baby, thought Elijah as he got himself together and picked up from where he left off at. Twenty minutes later he was done with his sermon.

"The doors of the church is open! We have a new member whom we have to welcome to our church family!" Elijah was ready to leave. Karter and Deacon Townsend sat out the chairs for the invitation. Karter was still mad about the way Elijah had handled Cynthia.

"We welcome brotha Thomas Clemons as the newest member of our congregation!" Elijah waved for Thomas to come up. When Cynthia heard Thomas's name, she quickly turned around to see if the name lined up with her uncle who she hadn't seen since she was ten. Oh my God! That's my uncle! I thought he was dead, thought Cynthia as she watched Thomas walk up to the front of the

Sinful Behavior

church and take a seat in the chair in front of Karter. Thomas looked at Cynthia with a smile on his face, then he placed his finger over his lips, telling Cynthia to not say anything. Thomas knew that Cynthia was the only person in the church who knew who he was. Cynthia couldn't believe her eyes.

Nobody else came up to be saved or join the church so Elijah had everyone to line up and shake Thomas's hand to welcome him into the church family. Thomas rubbed the back of Tasha's hand when he shook her hand. Elijah seen what he done, and he got mad, but Tasha was in front of him now and she had his undivided attention.

"Baby please come back into my life!" Elijah told Tasha as he shook her hand. His eyes were begging.

"Come over mama's house when you leave here!" Tasha said loud enough for everyone within ten feet of her to hear.

"I'm on my way now!" Elijah didn't care who or what anybody cared at the very moment. The hell with this, thought Elijah as he left the line to go to his office. When Cynthia made it to Thomas, she gave him a hug. Why is she hugging him, thought Karter. Thomas looked at the expression on Karter's face and he laughed.

"You and Thomas meet me and Samantha at Glady's Knight's Chicken and Waffle in thirty minutes!" Cynthia told Karter while she shook his hand.

"Okay! We'll be there!" Karter told her then Cynthia and Samantha left. Several church members tried to talk to Thomas, but Karter had to let them know that he couldn't talk. After the hand shaking was over, they left to go meet Cynthia and Samantha.

****

Tasha pulled into Coretta's driveway and before she could put her car in park Elijah pulled in behind her. Awe look at him! He been missin mama, thought Tasha as she looked in her rear-view mirror. She stepped out of her car and by the time she stood up, Elijah was in her face.

"Why did you do me like that baby?" Elijah looked like a sick puppy. Lights, camera, action, thought Tasha as she looked Elijah in the eyes. Then she made a tear run from her eye.

"You haven't thought for one minute about the way you've did me. You damn sholl ain't took into consideration what I've been going through in my life!"

Sinful Behavior

Tasha wiped her face and took off towards the front door of the house.

"Baby wait! Tasha! Hold up!" Elijah tried to stop Tasha, but she went into the house. Elijah went to the door and rang the doorbell. He couldn't just march into Coretta's house unannounced.

"What have you did to my child for her to be crying like she's about to die?" Coretta yelled at Elijah when she opened the door.

"Mama, I just asked her why did she do me like that, that's all!" Elijah tried to explain.

"Well it sure in the hell doesn't look like it! Now you need to go apologize to my baby!" Coretta was with the bullshit. Tasha came into the den and sat on the couch.

"Tasha, baby I'm sorry!" Elijah fell down in front of Tasha on his knees.

"I never meant to hurt you baby in any type of way!" Elijah pleaded.

"I can't do this Elijah! I can't, go home to your wife!" Tasha didn't mean one word of what she had just said, but Elijah didn't know that.

"I don't want anybody, but you baby! I swear I love you!"

"Elijah, you don't love me! You don't even know me!" Oh shit! Shit's about to hit the fan, thought Coretta as she watched her daughter play the game like a real "G".

"I know enough Tasha!" Elijah tried, but Tasha shook her head.

"You don't know shit, Elijah! You don't know that I was raped when I was thirteen! You don't know that I'm a fuckin stripper! You don't know I lived with a drug lord in Miami that I had to testify on in order not to do life in prison! You don't know that's the reason that I'm back in Atlanta!" Tasha talked real calm. Elijah was lost for words because he'd just got the story that he didn't know about. He searched for the right words to say as he stared in Tasha's eyes.

"That's what the fuck I thought!" Tasha said as she stood up from the couch. Elijah grabbed her by the arm and snatched her back down to her seat.

"None of that matters to me Tasha! That's your past! I love you!" Elijah leaned up and kissed Tasha on her lips. My baby is the butt naked truth! I might've taught that heifer a lil too much, thought Coretta as she watched the pastor submit to her daughters love spell.

"You mean that bay?" Tasha asked when she broke their kiss.

"Yes baby! We're gonna go find us somewhere to live tomorrow!"

"Baaaay!" Tasha jumped off the couch onto Elijah, causing him to fall back on the floor. Tasha laid on top of him and started kissing all over him. She was happier than a sissy in a football locker room.

****

"Hey sis! What you up to?" Thomas asked Pam as he clocked out from his job at the Mercedes Benz plant where he had just got promoted to supervisor and the rest of the night off.

"Oh, nothing brother! Just got done doing Cynthia's hair for her school play tomorrow! What's up?" Pam could hear happiness in her lil brothers voice.

"I just got a promotion at my job and we found out that we're having twins. A boy and a girl! I got off early, so I'm headed home to surprise Vanessa with the good news!" Thomas couldn't wait to deliver the news to his fiancé. To make the news even more significant he was gonna pick up a dozen roses and a Red Velvet cake from Kroger's.

"TC, that's great! Congratulations! I'm proud of you! I wish Paul was here so I could tell him the good news!" Pam was happy for her baby brother.

"Thanks sis! I'll talk to you later! I gotta swing by Kroger's to get Vanessa her favorite cake!" Thomas jumped into his Maxima.

"Now that I know that you're having twins, I can start shopping tomorrow!" Pam was happy that new family members were being born since Thomas was the only relative that she had alive by her parents.

"Okay, love! Later!" Thomas hung up as he pulled out of the plants parking lot. He was on cloud nine from having one of the best days of his life. He went by Kroger's where he grabbed a cake, some fruit and a few other things. Then he went home. Thomas was about to call Vanessa when he pulled up in front of their building, but that would've took away the surprise. When he stepped into his apartment the lights were off and Thomas could hear the sounds of R. Kelly's "Half On A Baby" playing in his bedroom. Pam must've called and told her that I was on my way home, thought Thomas as he sat the bags on the kitchen table. He took the roses out of the bag and held them while he went towards his bedroom. From down the hall he could tell the bedroom light was on. Thomas turned to walk in the bedroom, but he got frozen in his tracks. The entire room became red when Thomas saw Paul kissing on his fiancé's pregnant belly. Paul and Vanessa were so caught up in the moment, neither of them saw Thomas standing in the doorway. Paul kissed up Vanessa's pregnant stomach to her breast and took her nipple into his mouth. Then Paul stood up to take off his clothes. Thomas dropped the roses to the floor.

"Arrrrgh!" Thomas yelled to the top of his lungs as he ran at Paul, who was a way bigger man than Thomas.

"Get off me, punk!" Paul grabbed Thomas by his throat and threw him against the wall, knocking him windless.

"No, Paul! Don't hurt him! Just leave!" Screamed Vanessa as she jumped up from the bed, wrapping a robe around her naked body. Paul left out of the apartment before Thomas could muster up the strength to get up from the floor. Thomas got up and ran to the front door to try to catch Paul, but he was getting inside his car to leave. Thomas ran back to the bedroom.

"Bitch! I'ma kill you!!!!!" Thomas screamed as he wrapped his hands around Vanessa's neck and blanked out. When Thomas came back to reality it was too late. Vanessa and the kids in her stomach were dead. Pam was his only living family member and she didn't want anything to do with him when he went to jail. Pam told Thomas that she didn't want anything to do with him nor was she about to lose her husband for his bullshit allegations. Pam put a block on her phone, therefore Thomas couldn't call her house. 24 years later Thomas got his case overturned due to the law "Crime of Passion".

Thomas had been lost in his thoughts the entire ride to the restaurant to meet Cynthia and Samantha. He followed Karter inside the restaurant. Cynthia stood up from the table when she saw Thomas and Karter coming in her direction.

"Uncle Thomas!" Cynthia and Thomas hugged. Karter was lost and completely caught off guard by their actions. What? Uncle Thomas! Thought Karter as he stared at them hugging. When they let go of one another Karter noticed that Thomas was crying. Thomas sat down at the table and looked at Samantha, who looked just like Paul and Pam. He buried his face into his hands and the reality of what he did to Vanessa flashed into his brain. Cynthia put her arms around Thomas's shoulder while he cried.

"It's gonna be okay unc, I promise everything will be okay!" Cynthia assured Thomas. Karter sat down at the table next to Samantha. When Thomas raised his head and wiped his face, Karter got a real good look at him. That's when it all came together for Karter.

"TC! Is that you?" Thomas looked at Karter and nodded his head yes. Karter couldn't believe he had been around TC for weeks and he didn't know who he was. Thomas used to babysit Karter and Cynthia together when they were 8 and 9.

Thomas stood up and walked over to Samantha. He kissed her on the forehead, then he looked at Karter.

"Treat my niece right! She deserves a good man!" Thomas ran out of the restaurant without looking back before anyone could stop him.

"What the fuck? He can talk!" Karter was shocked.

"Of course, he can talk!" Cynthia knew why Thomas ran out of the restaurant and she also knew that would probably be the last time she seen him.

"Do you wanna tell me what's going on?" Karter was lost and he wanted answers.

Cynthia told Karter everything that she'd knew. Karter sat in awe while he learned about Thomas catching Pastor Dawson at his home with his pregnant fiancé. Cynthia told him the reason Thomas doesn't talk is because his family wouldn't talk to him when he went to prison for the murder and he still hadn't forgiven himself for what he'd done.

After Cynthia filled Karter in on Thomas, they ate their meals. Karter even had a talk with Samantha about men and life in general. Cynthia cried as she watched Karter be a father to her daughter.

"Mom, can you and Uncle Karter hook-up? I think he will make the perfect stepdad!" Samantha smiled. Cynthia looked at Karter then back to Samantha.

"I think he will too baby!"

****

Sinful Behavior

Yesterday Elijah wasn't about to let Tasha out of his eyesight, therefore he ended up spending the night with her at Coretta's house. When they woke up the following morning Elijah had his mind set on proving to Tasha that he wanted her and only her. He asked Tasha to ride with him to his house so he could get some clothes. When they pulled up in the driveway Tasha was astounded. She knew Elijah was living good, but she didn't know how good. Elijah was glad to see that everyone was gone when he opened the garage. He left Tasha in the car while he ran in the house to get enough clothes for a week. After throwing his outfits in an overnight bag, Elijah left out of the room and went downstairs. When he reached the bottom stair, Tasha was standing in the den looking around admiring the house.

"This is a very nice house Elijah! Are you sure that you wanna leave this to shack up in something that can't compare?" Tasha thought of herself as the master of reverse psychology. After seeing this, ain't no way in hell I'm bout to settle for anything less, thought Tasha as she looked at the family portrait standing on top of the fireplace.

Michael "Oodoo" Smith

"What do you mean, shack up in something that can't compare?" Tasha's question threw Elijah for a loop, causing wrinkles to appear across his forehead.

"Just what I said! You must finna get us something nice like this to move in!" Tasha's ratchetness appeared in full effort. She wasn't about to settle for less. She wanted to be spoiled.

"Yeah baby, I'm gonna get us something nice! Come on!" I gotta get out of here before someone sees her in here, thought Elijah. Yes, thought Tasha happy to hear that she was about to be living lavishly.

****

Thomas stepped off of the prison transport bus more nervous than an American Spy that had been captured by North Korean soldiers. With his wrist and ankles shackled, Thomas walked behind the convict in front of him while they were led into Hayes Maximum Security Prison in Georgia, which was filled with murderers, kidnappers and rapist.

"Inmate 422150, step on the X!" Thomas heard the CO call his number, so he stepped up on the X. The CO

Sinful Behavior

uncuffed his hands and feet. Then the CO led Thomas to his housing unit.

"Fresh meat!"

"What's up baby girl!"

"Damn she's fine!"

Thomas trembled on the inside from all of the taunting as he walked the corridor. He was glad that the men yelling at him were locked behind the cell doors.

"Roll door 75!" The CO said into his radio and the door to the cell Thomas was going inside opened up.

"Here bulldog! I got something for ya! Get in there bay!" The white CO ordered Thomas. Bulldog stood up from his rack standing 6 feet 5 inches and weighing 300 plus with Aryan brotherhood tattoos on his bald head.

"Special delivery, huh!" Bulldog looked like he was ready to eat Thomas.

"Yep! Just for you! He likes killing pregnant women, so you'll like him!" The white racist CO pushed Thomas's frail body into the cell, then shut and locked the door.

Michael "Oodoo" Smith

"Hmmm! Well boy you know what time it is, don't ya! It's either blood on my knife or shit on my dick!" Bulldog pulled out a jailhouse shank from his pants pocket. Thomas knew that this was gonna happen because some OG's in the county jail had told him so. Thomas threw his mat on the floor and got on his knees. Here goes nothing, thought Thomas.

"Do you want me to suck it first?" Thomas smiled. Bulldog smiled as he looked down at Thomas.

"Hmmm! I got me a lil nigger bitch, huh! Well since that's the case! Yeah, suck this white dick, nigger boy!" Bulldog sat his shank on the sink and pulled his pants down around his ankles. Bulldog smiled as Thomas reached up, grabbed his dick and started stroking it with his hand.

"Put it in your mouth! Nigger boy!" Bulldog demanded. Thomas guided Bulldog's dick towards his mouth and then flicked the blade from under his tongue. Thomas grabbed the blade and quickly sliced off Bulldog's dick.

"Arrrrrggghhhh!"

Sinful Behavior

"Huhm, hm, hmmm!" Thomas jumped up from out of his sleep, sweating from the nightmare he was having about the arrival of his trip to prison. The bed was soaking wet from the way he sweated while he dreamed.

"Huhm, huhm!" Thomas started crying and punching on the bed. He would do anything to have his fiancé back. Every day he lived made him regret his past more and more.

"Give me one more week baby and I'm coming to join you in the afterlife!" Thomas said through his tears.

****
***

Karter had been thinking about Cynthia all day, but even more so he'd been thinking about Thomas. He'd tried to call Thomas several times yesterday, but Thomas didn't answer. Karter was really concerned about Thomas and really wanted to know if he could help him in any type of way.

Karter finished the paperwork on the car he'd just sold then he clocked out for the day to go home. Cynthia was supposed to meet him at his condo at 3 o'clock.

Traffic was moving slow, so he called her phone to see where she was at, but she didn't answer. Good, thought when she didn't pick up. His phone began vibrating before he could sit it down, but it wasn't Cynthia. It was Patience a military girl that Karter and Elijah had ran a train on and occasionally used her for her good sex. She had been calling Karter all day, but he had yet to talk to her. Fuck, what does she want, thought Karter as he answered the phone.

"What do you want, Patience?" Karter hated for someone to be so worrisome.

"What do you mean, what do I want? I'm five months pregnant with your child!" Karter almost hit the car in front of him when he heard Patience.

"You're crazy as hell! That ain't my baby!" Karter hung up on Patience.

"Crazy ass woman done slept with me, Elijah and ain't no tellin who else, but you gonna try to put it on me!" Karter said out loud while he was glad to see that traffic was speeding up some. He tried to call Cynthia, but he still didn't get an answer. Good! I need to get my thoughts together anyways, thought Karter. Ten minutes later he pulled into the parking garage of the building where his condo was located. When he reached his parking space, he damn near had an anxiety attack when he saw Cynthia and Patience standing outside of their cars conversating with one another.

"Mane, Fuck!" Karter said unconsciously as he parked.

"I told you he would be pulling up in a minute, didn't I girl?" Cynthia smiled at Karter as he approached them.

"What are you doing here, Patience?" Damn she is pregnant, thought Karter as he looked at her stomach.

"Because I'm pregnant!" Patience started crying and fell onto Cynthia's shoulder.

"Don't do this poor young lady like that!" Cynthia's words were full of sarcasm! Karter shook his head in disbelief.

"Come on inside!" What all does Cynthia know thought Karter as he led the way to his Condo.

"So, Patience! You are saying that you're pregnant by me!" Karter his keys onto the kitchen island as he went to the fridge to get himself a cold beer.

"Yes! I'm pregnant by you or either Elijah. I've sent him messages and called his phone, but he won't talk to me!" Patience spilled the beans. Cynthia smirked and shook her head.

"Patience, baby how old are you?" Cynthia could tell that Patience was young.

"I'm 21!"

"And how old were you when you first engaged in sex with Karter, Elijah or both of them?"

"When I was nineteen!" She answered! Cynthia looked at Karter and if looks could've killed, he would've been dead.

"Listen Patience, baby! I want you to know that no matter if Karter or Elijah is the father of your child, your child will be taken care of regardless and I'm gonna make sure of that! Put my number in your phone!" Patience took out her phone and logged in Cynthia's number.

"I leave next week to go to Huntsville, Alabama, where I'm stationed at!" Patience informed Cynthia.

Sinful Behavior

"Girl, call me tomorrow so we can go out to eat and start planning for you a baby shower!" Cynthia put a big smile on Patience's face.

"Come on! I'll walk you to the door and don't ever worry about no, no good ass man anymore! Don't love nobody, but yourself and your baby!" Cynthia shot her eyes in Karter's direction. He stood speechless, shaking his head while he watched Cynthia handle the situation.

"Thanks Cynthia!"

"You're welcome Boo! Call me tomorrow!" Cynthia and Patience hugged. Then Patience looked at Karter.

"Fuck you! You lil dick bastard!" Patience screamed at Karter as she shot him the middle finger right before she left out of his condo and slammed the door.

"Uhm, uhm, uhm!" Cynthia shook her head at Karter.

"Cynt! I don't know what all she told you, but she's...!" Karter tried to say, but Cynthia cut him short.

"Karter, don't you try to sit here and tell me that, that young girl lied to me while I was sitting outside waiting on you. She pulled up next to me crying and I just so happened to roll my window down to ask her if she was okay. That's when she started telling me, a complete stranger about how Pastor Elijah Woods and Deacon Karter Jones ran a damn train on her at this very location. So, before you fix your lips to speak, please choose your words wisely or this may just be our last time speaking!" Cynthia crossed her arms and waited for Karter to respond. Karter took a deep breath.

"You right, beautiful! She isn't lying and there is a possibility that Elijah is the father because I wore a condom, but he couldn't fit the size that I wear, so he just went bareback with her. And just to be honest with you, she's not the only female that we have had sexual encounters with. Baby I don't wanna live like that anymore. I'm too old for this shit!" Karter flopped down on the couch and put his head in his hands. Cynthia sat her purse down on the table and then she stood in front of Karter.

"You promise me that you are done with your past life! Cause if not, I understand, and we can just be friends' baby!" Cynthia ran her fingers through Karter's dreads. Karter took his hands off his face and now he was looking

Sinful Behavior

at Cynthia's gorgeous French pedicured feet that sat inside the Jimmy Choo sandals she was wearing. He slick had a foot fetish. Karter's eyes traveled from her feet, up her smooth legs. He had been so discombobulated since the moment he drove up and seen Patience talking to Cynthia that he was just now realizing that Cynthia had on a sun dress when his eyes met her thighs.

"I promise baby! I don't want nothing but you!" Said Karter as he rubbed Cynthia's thigh. She raised up her dress showing Karter that she didn't have on no panties. Slob ran from Karter's mouth as he stared at Cynthia's pretty pussy. Her spur tongue peaked at Karter through the lips of her pretty bald pussy. Cynthia turned around putting her back to Karter, then she bent over and grabbed her ankles causing Karter's vision to be filled with nothing but asshole and pussy. He didn't hesitate to stick his tongue out and lick Cynthia's passion fruit.

"Ahhhh baaaaby!" Cynthia moaned as Karter spread her ass cheeks further apart and constantly flicked his tongue across her clitoris.

"Your lil freaky ass like that, don't you?" Karter said between licks. The way he talked to Cynthia drove her crazy and made her pussy flow like the Nile River. Karter stuck his two fingers into her boiling hot pussy.

"Ummm, hmm!" Cynthia moaned as she put one hand on the table in front of her for balance then she reached around the back of her. Cynthia grabbed the hand of the fingers Karter was penetrating inside of her and pulled his fingers out of her pussy. Then she guided his wet fingers to her asshole.

"Damn baby! That's where you want it?" Karter asked softly. Cynthia grabbed his fingers and penetrated them into her asshole. Karter watched as she slid his fingers in and out.

"I want you to put that dick in my ass!" Cynthia pulled his fingers out of her asshole, then she stood up and pulled her sun dress off.

"Do you got some baby oil?" She asked Karter.

"Yeah! Under the sink in the bathroom!" Damn, I'm about to get my first shot of ass! Oohwee, thought Karter as he stood up from the couch and got naked. That lil hard muthafucka oughta feel real good in my ass, thought Cynthia when she laid eyes on Karter's hard dick as she walked back into the den holding a bottle of Johnson and Johnson baby oil.

"Here!" Cynthia handed Karter the baby oil then she got on the couch in a doggy style position. Cynthia spread her ass cheeks as Karter got behind her.

"Lube that ass and stick that dick in baby!" Cynthia demanded Karter, feenin to feel his dick inside of her. Karter squeezed the baby oil all over Cynthia's asshole then he sat the bottle down. Next, he placed the head of his rock-hard dick at her asshole and began pushing it inside of Cynthia.

"Ummm, yesss Kaaaarter!" Cried Cynthia when she felt the head of Karter's dick penetrate her insides. Karter took his time slowly easing dick a little at a time like he had seen it done on pornos.

Smack!

"Harder baby!" Cynthia screamed for Karter to slap her ass harder.

Smack! Smack! Smack!

"Like that baby!" Karter asked Cynthia while he appreciated the way her asshole gripped his dick tightly.

Cynthia let go of her ass cheeks and began rubbing on her clit.

"Ahh, ahh, ooh yess Kaarrrter!" Cynthia felt her orgasm coming hard. Karter started pounding her asshole like it was a pussy.

"Ooh Cyynt! This ass feels sooo good!" Karter was loving his first anal sex experience.

"I'mmm cummmmiiinnnn!" Cynthia screamed and her body started jerking, but Karter mounted her asshole even harder.

"Ahhhh shit baby! I'mm bout to bust!"

"Nut in that ass, Daddy!" Cynthia wanted to feel Karter's warm sperm inside of her asshole.

"Huhh, hugh, crrghh!" Karter's knees buckled as he shot semen inside of Cynthia's ass. The feeling of his warm sperm fluids getting sprayed inside of her sent Cynthia into another orgasm.

"Kaaarrrteeerrr!" Cynthia sang as she came again. Karter tried to keep stroking her insides, but it was impossible. He was to weak and his dick was not hard enough to stay in her ass. Damn! That was the best sex

Sinful Behavior

ever, thought Karter as he laid back on the couch to catch his breath. Cynthia turned around and climbed up on his chest trying to control her breathing in the process. Karter rubbed his fingers through her soft silky hair while they laid in silence listening to each other breathing for a few minutes.

"Cynt!" Karter broke the silence.

"Yes baby!" Cynthia ran her fingernails across Karter's muscular chest.

"I've been thinking, and I came up with the conclusion that I'm gonna tell Elijah about us!" Karter was in love and he wasn't gonna be creeping around hiding from anybody. Cynthia raised up and looked Karter in the eyes, smiling.

"Baby, I want you to be sure about you wanting to be with me!" Cynthia had to be sure that Karter wasn't playing with her.

"I'm positive about what I wanna do, but are you sure, since you telling me to be sure!" Karter smiled, but his smile quickly disappeared when he seen Cynthia's eyes water up and a tear ran down her face.

Michael "Oodoo" Smith

"I can't afford another heartbreak!" Cynthia said sniffling.

"Baby you in good hands with Allstate!" Said Karter and they burst into laughter.

Karter and Cynthia cuddled for the next hour while they became more familiar with one another. Then Cynthia cooked dinner and invited Samantha and Jr. over to eat with them. She wanted for her kids to express how they felt about her decision to be in a relationship with Karter, the man who they had known as their fathers' best friend for almost their entire lives.

When the kids made it over, they all ate. Then Karter talked to Jr. about his sexual preference. He let Jr. know that he shouldn't be ashamed of his sexuality and told him to practice safe sex. Jr. was overwhelmed with joy from the advice and motivation that Karter had given him. Cynthia shed tears as she watched Karter give her son life lessons that his own father wouldn't take the time out to do. Samantha didn't make the situation any better when she got ready to leave, she called Karter, dad. It was as if the kid couldn't depart the condo fast enough, because as soon as the door closed behind the kids, Karter and Cynthia tore into one another making love all night.

Sinful Behavior

Michael "Oodoo" Smith

CHAPTER 7

Elijah didn't show up at church Tuesday, Wednesday, Thursday, Friday, nor did he show up for his basketball game on Saturday. He had been so busy spoiling Tasha that he hadn't thought about anything else besides making her happy. Several members of the Deacon and Mothers board had called him asking was he okay and he told them all that he was out of town handling business. They knew Pastor Woods was lying because most of them were mutual friends on Facebook and Instagram with Coretta Caine who reposted almost everything Tasha posted. Everyone knew about the new Benz and the two-bedroom condo Elijah had bought Tasha. The congregation couldn't believe how their pastor was spending money like crazy on a woman that wasn't his wife. Elijah's name was becoming the topic of many conversations and it wasn't in a good way, therefore the members of the church board decided that they should have a meeting to discuss the pastor's actions.

Elijah and Tasha had spent the entire Saturday shopping for furniture and other odds and ends for their new condo, so they decided to go eat dinner at Ruth Chris. They had just got seated when Elijah's phone rang. It was Karter so Elijah rejected the call like he had been doing all week. Then another phone call came in and it was Reverend Darius Williams, a young and upcoming pastor from St. Paul Baptist Church. Elijah answered the call.

"Pastor Williams! God bless you! How are you doing?" Said Elijah.

"Oh, I'm fine brother! And how about yourself Pastor Woods?"

"Any better and I'd be sitting next to Jesus Christ himself!" Elijah smiled at Tasha. Then he leaned over and kissed her.

"That's good to hear! I was just calling to inform you that my entire congregation will be attending the service tomorrow since I'm the guest speaker for the Pastor's Anniversary Service!" Elijah felt like someone had hit him across the head with a hammer. How in the hell did I forget that tomorrow is my anniversary, thought Elijah as he held his phone to his ear with his mouth gaped open.

"Hello! Pastor Woods!" Said Reverend Williams when the phone got quiet.

"Oh yes! Yes reverend, I can't wait for you to bring the word with you tomorrow! I'll see you when you get there!" Elijah shook his head in awe.

"Okay pastor! Take it easy!" Reverend Williams hung up.

"Who was that baby?" Tasha asked being nosey.

"That was Pastor Williams from St. Paul! What are you gonna order!" Elijah changed the subject.

"Elijah, I know there's something on your mind! So, what is it?" Tasha saw that Elijah was worried about something because he wasn't acting the same after he talked to whoever he was talking to on the phone. Elijah took a deep breath.

"Tomorrow's my Pastor's Anniversary!" Elijah shook his head.

"Uhmm, so I guess that means you and your wife gotta be the perfect, loving married couple tomorrow!" Tasha twisted up her face and Elijah remained silent.

Sinful Behavior

"You know what? I'm not even hungry anymore! Take me home!" Tasha got up from the table and marched out of the restaurant. If it ain't one thing then it's a damn notha, thought Elijah as he got up from the table to leave. The entire ride to Tasha's new condo was silent.

"You can go home to your family!" Tasha told Elijah as soon as they pulled into the parking garage.

"I'm at where I wanna be!" Elijah got out of the car and walked towards the elevator. Oh, he think I'm playin wit his ass, thought Tasha as she followed behind Elijah.

"Go home to your bitch Elijah! That's who you gotta be with tomorrow at church!" Tasha said as they rode the elevator.

Ding!

"I know you hear me!" Tasha screamed as they got off the elevator, but Elijah ignored her. Elijah opened the door to the condo and walked inside.

"I said go home to your bitch!" Tasha got in Elijah's face. I gotta show this bitch who's the man, thought Elijah and he grabbed Tasha by her shoulders and threw her onto the futon couch. Tasha swung her hands wildly at Elijah, but she didn't hit him hard. Take this pussy nigga! Make me know that you're my man, thought Tasha as she acted as if she wanted to fight, but she really wanted to fuck. Elijah saw the lust behind Tasha's anger, and he knew exactly what she wanted.

"Shut the fuck up!" Elijah growled as he pulled up Tasha's skirt, which she had on no panties beneath.

"Get off me!" Tasha barely tried pushing Elijah off of her while she tried to sound convincing, but her vagina was wet as the Indian Ocean. That's it Daddy! Take this pussy, thought Tasha as she watched Elijah unbuckle his pants and pull his dick out.

"I said shut the fuck up!" Elijah put one hand over Tasha's mouth then he shoved his cock into her splash pad.

"Hhmmm, hmm!" Tasha whimpered. Elijah took his hand off her mouth and grabbed her hair pulling the roots while he pumped her wishing well.

"Hahhhh, oooh, fuck mee!" Tasha moaned softly as she looked into Elijah's menacing eyes.

"Didn't I say shut the fuck up!" Elijah wrapped both of his hands around Tasha's throat and applied more pressure to her wind pipe while he long stroked her insides. Oh, my fuckin God! I love this nigga, thought Tasha as she felt her insides overheat while her eyes rolled back into her head.

"Ughhh! I'm cumminn!" Tasha managed to say as she creamed Elijah's dick with her thick nut. Elijah let go of her neck and pulled out of her pussy. He stood up and looked at Tasha while he pulled up his pants.

"I expect you to be at church tomorrow!" Elijah said as he buckled his pants.

"Okay Daddy! I love you!" Tasha had needed exactly what Elijah had just given her. He leaned down and kissed her on the lips.

"I love you too!" Elijah left.

I gotta tell Cynthia that I want a divorce. She can have the cars and the house, but she can't have any of my money, thought Elijah as he drove home. When he pulled into the driveway, he pushed the button on the garage opener, but the garage door didn't come up. Elijah parked, got out of the car and went to the front door. He stuck his key into the door, but it didn't fit. What the hell is going on, thought Elijah as he switched keys thinking that maybe he had the wrong one, but the other keys didn't work either. He pulled his phone out and called Cynthia.

Michael "Oodoo" Smith

"Hello!" She answered.

"Why doesn't my key work to the front door and the garage opener ain't working neither?"

"Probably because I had my locks changed, but I'm sure your keys work to where you've been all week!" Elijah couldn't believe the way Cynthia was talking to him.

"You better let me in my fuckin house, bitch!" Elijah growled then he kicked the front door.

"My lawyer will contact you Monday about our divorce. I'm sure you'll be happy with Tasha!" Cynthia smirked then she hung up on Elijah.

Boom

Elijah kicked in the front door and ran upstairs to his bedroom, but nobody was in there.

"Where you at, bitch?" Elijah stormed through the house looking for anybody, but nobody was there. When he looked in the garage, he saw Cynthia's and Jr.'s car was gone.

****

Tara's parents, Deyonda and Tevin Giles pulled out of their driveway to go to an all-white party that they had gotten invited to by some friends of theirs. There was plenty for a senior in high school to do, but Tara wanted to stay at home on a Saturday to study for her upcoming exams. Tara's 4.1 G.P.A. had all the top colleges in the country trying to give her a full scholarship to their school. After studying for an hour, Tara decided to take a shower. Twenty minutes later she stepped out of the shower reaching for her towel.

Now I know I put my towel right there, thought Tara as she noticed that her towel wasn't where she had put it. She walked to the bathroom closet to get another towel. After she wrapped her body in the towel, she stepped into the hallway.

Swoosh!

"Huu, huu, hu!" Tara gagged for air while she struggled to breathe from the plastic bag that was over her head. She clawed and scratched at her predator, but it didn't do her any good. Her attacker dragged her into her bedroom, picked her up and threw her onto the bed. Tara poked a hole in the bag as soon as she hit the bed.

"Stop! Huu, huu, please stop! Huu, hu!" Tara screamed between breathes. Then she snatched the bag from off of her head.

"Huu, huu! What's goin on?" Tara said out loud when she saw that nobody was in the room with her. She quickly scrambled to her phone that was on the nightstand charging and she called her dad.

"Hello! Hello!" Tevin screamed over the music playing in the background.

"Daddy hurry up come home! Somebody broke into our house and attacked me!" Cried Tara. She was scared to death.

"Baby call the police on three-way! I'm on my way right now. Tevin and Deyonda left the party immediately. By the time they made it home the police and detectives were already there along with a news crew. Tevin and Deyonda ran up to Tara and hugged her.

"What happened baby?" Tevin wanted to know.

"When I got out of the shower someone threw a plastic bag over my head then dragged me into my room and threw me onto my bed. I ripped the bag off my head and they were gone, but he left one of his shoes here and I must've tore his shirt while I was trying to fight him off because half of his shirt was on the floor!" Tevin and Deyonda could tell that their daughter was shook like hell from her encounter with the predator. The detectives walked up to them.

"Would any one of you happened to drop these business cards in the front yard!" Detective Robinson, a short, heavy set, black man asked them. Tevin, Deyonda and Tara all shook their heads no.

"Well do any of you know a Pastor Elijah Woods?" he asked them.

"Yes, that's our pastor!" Said Deyonda.

"Well, we're gonna try to see if we can get a DNA match off this shirt and shoe, but we may also pay your pastor a visit!" Detective Robinson pulled out his contact info.

"That's not possible! Our pastor wouldn't do this!" Tevin said as he looked at the yellow shoe and torn t-shirt inside the bag Detective Robinson was holding.

"You never know these days Mr. Giles! My shift is about to end, but I will be getting to work early tomorrow, so expect a call from me!" Detective Robinson gave Tevin his card with his number on it. Tevin, Deyonda and Tara watched as the scene cleared out. Within ten minutes they were home alone. They went into their den and sat down.

Deyonda had a weird look on her face and Tevin sensed that there was something wrong with her. He knew his wife of 17 years.

"Baby why are you looking like that?" Tevin asked Deyonda.

"Um! I'm just thinking! Nothin!" Deyonda shook her head.

"What baby? What are you just thinking?" Tevin threw his hands in the air. He hated when Deyonda didn't speak her mind. Deyonda looked at him.

"I think I do remember seeing Pastor Woods with those ugly yellow shoes on!" Deyonda nodded her head up and down.

"Are you sure baby?" Tevin felt his anger rising.

"We'll just wait to see what the detective finds out baby! I don't wanna jump to any conclusions! Now come on and let's get a shower!" Deyonda was almost a hundred percent sure about what she said, but she didn't want Tevin to do anything stupid.

****

Sinful Behavior

At 9 A.M. Elijah parked his GLE in his reserved parking spot in front of the church. There were a few cars sitting in the parking lot when he arrived. Thomas was one of them. Elijah stepped out of his SUV wearing a off white Steve Harvey Collection Suite with the matching throwback Stacy Adams on his feet. He was smiling from the facetime conversation him and Tasha was having before he got out of his vehicle. Elijah walked up to the front door and unlocked it, then he went to his office, where he remained alone until 9:45 AM when Pastor Williams and his wife came inside. They talked for thirty minutes while they ate a light breakfast before they made their way to the sanctuary. Pastor Williams seated his wife on the front row with the other Mothers of the church, then he joined Elijah in the pulpit.

Karter walked through the doors of the sanctuary looking like new money in a olive-green three-piece Ralph Lauren dress suit with the matching olive-green Louboutins on his feet. He spoke to several members of both churches and gave a few hugs as he made his way to his seat in the Deacon's section. As soon as Karter sat down, he saw Tasha and Coretta Caine walking down the aisle. Tasha's soft purple and gold Kim Wooo dress, which everyone who followed her on social media knew that Elijah had purchased because she had posted it on Facebook, was so tight that if she ate a York Peppermint Patty the threads were gonna break.

Why is she sitting on the front row with the Mothers of the church, thought Karter as he watched Tasha sit next to Coretta and Pastor William's wife. Where is Thomas? Karter asked himself as he looked around knowing that he'd seen the caddy parked front and center when he pulled up in the parking lot.

The organ players started playing and the choir began singing as the service began. Elijah smiled when he saw Elijah Jr. walk in with one of his friends and sit near the front. Oh shit, thought Karter when he saw Jr., who spoke to him. Karter threw his hand up speaking back to Jr. After the choir finished their song everyone stood up and began walking towards the altar to donate their tithes and offering to the collection box.

Tara and Kendra stood up from their seats and walked to the front to put their offering into the plate, but Tara got frozen in her steps when she looked towards the pulpit and saw a yellow shoe identical to the shoe that the person who attacked her left at the house. Tara felt the hair on the back of her neck stand up, and chill bumps covered her skin. She turned around and ran to get her purse. Then she ran outside and called her mom.

"Hello!" Deyonda answered the phone.

"Mama! I just saw that same yellow shoe sitting next to the podium in the pulpit!" Tara looked around as if someone was chasing her.

"Calm down baby! I'm about to call the detective! Me and your daddy are on the way there, right now!" Deyonda hung up the phone and called Detective Robinson.

It's time for me to let my people know, thought Elijah as he listened to the choir sing. He knew it was time for him to confess to his congregation what they already knew because of Tasha's social media and the way he had been acting. Elijah wasn't about to lie or hide anything from his congregation. He stood up from his seat and began clapping to the music as he walked up to the podium after he seen Cynthia and Samantha walk into the sanctuary.

"God is good!" Elijah screamed out loud. A few members rose to their feet and started praising God with Elijah.

"I said my God is good!" Elijah screamed as he pointed to the sky. Look at my baby, thought Tasha with a Kool-Aid smile on her face. Elijah Jr. got up from his seat and walked up to the altar. Then fell to his knees.

"Lord give me the strength I need to be who I really am! Lord please love me for me and forgive me for my sins! Amen!" Jr. prayed. Elijah smiled at his son. Elijah Jr. walked up to the pulpit where his dad was at grabbed the microphone and walked back down by the altar. What is he doing, thought Elijah as he watched his son signal to the organ player for him to stop playing the organ.

"Hi everybody! I'm the pastor's son and I would like a moment of your time if you don't mind!" Said Jr. when the music stopped, but then he felt a lump in his throat, and it became hard for him to swallow. Elijah seen that his son needed his support, so he left the pulpit and went and put his arm around Jr.'s shoulder.

"Go ahead son! Say whatever God wants you to say! Your father is here to support you!" Elijah motivated Jr. A tear fell out of Jr.'s eye so he looked at his father. Then he looked over at Jason and waved for him to come stand beside him. When Jason made it beside Jr., they locked hands, which made wrinkles spread across Elijah's face.

"I want everyone to know that I'm gay and this is Jason my boyfriend. We plan on getting married!" Elijah Jr. proudly announced with a smile on his face. A mug of defeat covered Elijah's face. He couldn't believe what had just come out of his son's mouth.

BOOM!

The sanctuary doors swung open, hitting the walls hard demanding everyone's attention. Detective Robinson and two uniformed cops marched down the aisle, walking straight up to Elijah.

"You have the right to remain silent…." The uniformed cops slammed Elijah onto the floor and detained him while Detective Robinson read him his rights. Elijah had no notion to what was going on. Detective Robinson retrieved the yellow shoe from the pulpit.

BOOM!

The doors of the sanctuary flew open again with Tevin flying down the aisle like a superhero with Deyonda on his heels. The cops got Elijah to his feet.

Michael "Oodoo" Smith

"I'm gonna kill you, you punk muthafucka!" Screamed Tevin.

Bing Pow Bing

Tevin hit Elijah with a three-piece combo to the face. The police had to detain Tevin and put him in cuffs. Tasha ran to Elijah's side.

"Baby what's going on?" Cried Tasha out loud.

"Baby I don't know!" Screamed Elijah.

"Oh, you know you punk bitch! You tried to rape my daughter!" Tevin yelled loud enough for the people riding by the church to hear.

"Oh shit!"

"Did you hear that?"

"Pastor Woods is a rapist!"

"We gotta find a new church!" The members of the congregation started saying all types of things as they watched Pastor Woods be hauled out of the church in handcuffs. Elijah looked at Samantha as he passed the last row. He was so ashamed that he dropped his head, but not before he saw the big smile on Cynthia's face while she recorded the entire scene on her iPhone. This is crazy, thought Karter as he watched the chaos unravel right before his eyes. Karter felt someone tap him on his shoulder.

"Looks like it's your time to be pastor after you clean this mess up!" Deacon Sykes, the senior deacon and head of the church board told Karter.

"I don't know if I'm ready to do that!" Replied Karter.

"Well Pastor Jones, you might wanna get ready because the board has already voted you in!" Deacon Sykes patted Karter on the shoulder then he walked away on his walker.

Elijah stared into the camera lens of Channel 6 News as soon as he stepped outside the church. The misery and embarrassment of the day his brother beat him up and he had to go to school with two black eyes couldn't compare to the way Elijah was feeling at the very moment. When the police loaded him into the back of the police car, Elijah ducked his head down and tried to hide his face. He was so ashamed.

"Baby, what's going on?" Tasha cried outside the door of the police car, but her cry fell on deaf ears.

Michael "Oodoo" Smith

"Ma'am back away from the car!" The police ordered Tasha.

****

Karter hated to see Elijah go to jail. No matter how he felt about Cynthia, Elijah was still somewhat like a brother to him. He knew he had reached a point in his life where he had to choose between a relationship with Cynthia or a brotherhood with Elijah. Karter sat at the island inside his kitchen and threw back shots of Patron while he rationalized in his brain whether or not Elijah was capable of committing the crime that he was charged with.

Ring Ring Ring

Karter's doorbell rang. He got up to go see who was at his door but when he looked through the peephole no one was there. Karter opened the door and on the outside of the door was an envelope sitting on the doormat with a set of keys sitting on top of it. Karter quickly recognized that the keys were to his caddy. He picked up the keys and envelope, then he went sat down back at the island. Karter sat the keys down and pulled the letter out of the unsealed envelope:

Dear Karter,

Sinful Behavior

What's up bruh or should I say nephew? Lol! Do me a favor and take good care of my niece. She deserves a good man. I couldn't stand to see Elijah's punk ass treat Cynthia like her father treated her mama, so I did something about it. Take that seat as pastor at that church and be the best damn pastor that you can be. The evidence to get Elijah out of jail is sitting above the visor in the caddy. Thanks for everything nephew, but tomorrow I must go see my wife and kids in the afterlife!

Love Uncle TC

Michael "Oodoo" Smith

CHAPTER 8

Jail was no place for anyone, but it definitely wasn't the place for Elijah. When he first made it to jail the police booked him in, then they put him in a one-man solitary confinement cell. Since Detective Robinson felt some type of way about the prominent young Pastor Woods trying to rape a young girl, he told the booking officers to leave Elijah in the one man until he got him out to interrogate him. Elijah went to sleep as soon as he got in the cell. The anxiety drained all of his energy. He woke up at four in the morning and wondered why he was still in the one man. He began pacing the cell. The screams of a crazy man in the cell next to him were driving him crazy.

How could anyone live in a place like this, thought Elijah as he looked at the tray of food that the police had slid through the slot in the cell door. The bologna was four different colors, the boiled egg was cold as ice and the toast wasn't toasted.

I can't believe they are actually charging me with burglary and assaulting Deyonda's daughter thought Elijah

Sinful Behavior

as he paced back and forth in the cold cell trying to keep warm. It seemed as if he'd been in jail for a month, but it had only been twenty hours. Thoughts of Tasha crying as the police carried him away flooded Elijah's brain. Tired of pacing the floor, Elijah sat down on his rack. He laid down on the thin mattress and tucked his arms into his shirt, but before he could get comfortable, Elijah jumped up when he heard keys unlocking his cell door.

"Elijah Woods! Step out of the cell!" Detective Robinson ordered Elijah. When Elijah stepped into the hall Detective Robinson put handcuffs and ankle restraints on him. Then Elijah followed Detective Robinson down the hall and into the interrogation room.

"Have a seat!" Elijah sat down at the table.

"You are charged with burglary and second-degree assault! Do you want to make a statement or do you wanna contact your lawyer?" Detective Robinson asked Elijah.

"I wanna talk to my lawyer!" Elijah said with his head down.

"Okay your bond is set at $30,000 cash bond! Come on so I can get you into population!"

Ring Ring

Michael "Oodoo" Smith

Detective Robinson's phone rang.

"Hello…. Okay…..I'm bringing him down now! Detective Robinson hung up his phone.

"Your attorney is here to talk to you!" He told Elijah. Then he took Elijah to the attorney's visiting room. Elijah never knew he would be so happy to see his lawyer Ms. Candriah Smothers in his life.

"Why the cuffs Robinson?" She asked knowing that Elijah was not supposed to be cuffed nor shackled.

"Oh, my bad! He looks like a runner!" Detective Robinson smirked then took his time uncuffing Elijah.

"How are you doing?" Candriah asked Elijah once Detective Robinson left the room.

"I managed to find hell on earth!" He replied as he massaged his wrists while he fought to hold back the tears that he so badly wanted to release.

"Hmm, I'm sorry to hear that!" Candriah grabbed a manilla envelope from her suitcase when she sat down at the table. Elijah sat down across from her.

"Look, Elijah! You're gonna have to excuse my French, but I'm not gonna bullshit you in any type of way!"

Candriah's vulgar language quickly put Elijah on the edge and grasped his attention.

"These charges are serious due to the fact that the victim is a minor and from what I've found out through my reliable sources, the police have clothes from the scene that they believe have your DNA on it! The family has put a protection order on you that has prevented you from bonding out and on top of everything, your wife's lawyer faxed me this last night!" Candriah took the papers out of the envelope and slid them to Elijah.

There were ten pictures clipped to the front papers. Elijah shook his head in disbelief as he looked at the first picture. The picture was of him and Tasha holding hands in Saks Fifth, inside the Lenoxx Mall. The next picture he looked at was of him and Tasha inside the condo he'd purchased for her.

"I thought maybe your wife had hired a private investigator or something to get the photos, but when I looked at Tasha Caine's Facebook and Snapchat, I saw some of these exact pictures. Elijah couldn't do anything but shake his head while he looked at the photos. Elijah sat the pictures down and looked at Candriah.

Michael "Oodoo" Smith

"So, what all does she want?" Elijah asked pertaining to the divorce papers.

"When I read over those papers her lawyer sent me, it seems like your wife wants everything, but your last name!" Candriah didn't sugar coat anything. A tear fell from Elijah's eye. He couldn't hold it in any longer. Cynthia's name is on everything! The house, the church, the cars and the bank accounts! Fuck! Thought Elijah as he sat speechless with his bottom lip quivering. Candriah got up from her seat and walked around the table to Elijah. She patted him on his shoulder.

"I'm gonna try to talk to the family to try to get the protection order lifted off you so you can bond out on house arrest or something. I'll be back tomorrow to see you. Be careful in there!" Candriah picked up all of her papers and left. A CO came and got Elijah to take him to population.

****

Cynthia had been calling and texting Karter for a whole twenty-four hours and he didn't have the decency to pick up or text her back. She was tired of being ignored by Karter, but she was fiening to get the itch she was having scratched by someone other than herself. Everybody must

Sinful Behavior

be mad or down cause Elijah in jail, but I'm not and to be honest I want some celebration sex, thought Cynthia as she decided to dial the number on the business card that she was holding in her hand. Her palms began to sweat as she held her phone while she listened to the phone ring.

Hang up the phone Cynthia! What are you thinking, Cynthia thought convincing herself to hang up the phone, but then she heard a voice on the other end.

"Dr. Feel Good speaking!" The baritone voice made Cynthia's pussy moist.

"Hi! Handsome!" Cynthia managed to nervously say while she felt a tingle between her thick thighs.

"Well, hi to you miss lady! May I ask whom I am speaking with?"

"This is the woman with the prettiest skin that you've ever seen!" Cynthia knew he would remember her.

"So, there is a God, huh! How are you doing beautiful?" An image of Cynthia instantly popped up in Dr. Feel Good's head.

"I'm not even gonna lie! I'm not doing too good that's why I called the doctor to see if he was in the Atlanta area! I could really use some special attention right now!" Cynthia twirled her hair.

"Just between me and you, beautiful I live here in Atlanta! Do you remember how to get to the house you came to for the live show that you attended in?"

"How could I ever forget the way?"

A hour later Cynthia pulled up to the gate of the mansion that she'd once visited before. She rolled down her window and pressed the speaker button on the intercom system.

"Yes, may I help you?" Said a woman's voice.

"Yes! I'm here to see Dr. feel Good!"

"Drive through the gate and walk up to the front door!" The woman instructed Cynthia who watched the gates open up. Cynthia got out of the car wearing a Blue Kim Wooo sundress with no panties on beneath it and a pair of six-inch Jimmy Choo heels. She walked to the door and rang the doorbell. Seconds later the same Brazilian woman who was laying in Dr. Feel Good's bed, answered the door wearing a white silk robe.

"Hi, I'm Suzanne! Come in!" She said smiling and waving her hand for Cynthia to come inside the house.

"I'm Cynthia!" I told him I needed some special attention! Why would he tell me to come here where there are lots of people at? Cynthia questioned herself as she followed Suzanne through the house.

"Would you like some Champagne or anything else?" Suzanne asked Cynthia who was about to answer her question, but when she turned to walk into the room, she lost her train of thought.

"Aaaaah fuuuuck meee haaaarderrrr!" Screamed the thick, big booty brown skinned girl that Dr. Feel Good was fucking in her ass with his huge king size snicker. Cynthia was amazed at how they were shooting an actual porn right in front of her.

"Spit in her asshole!" The director ordered Dr. feel Good. Damn! That shit looks painful, thought Cynthia as she watched the woman take all of the doctor in her ass.

"Okay! Now pull out and nut in her asshole for the camera!" Said the director. Wow thought Cynthia while she watched Dr. Feel Good bust a nut on command as the woman, he was fucking made her asshole breath in and out like a heaving chest.

"Okay cut! Good job Lovely!" The director was very satisfied with the way Lovely took the dick from Dr. Feel Good. He had plans on making her a star.

"No! That was a great job by the doctor!" Lovely giggled, wishing that the scene had never ended. Dr. Feel Good wrapped a towel around his waist then he walked up to Cynthia.

"Well, I'll be damned if it ain't Miss Pretty Skin herself!" Dr. Feel Good made Lovely feel some type of way by the way he was looking at Cynthia. Lovely rolled her eyes at Cynthia, but Cynthia didn't see her because her eyes was focused on the doctor's frame.

"Who do we have here?" Alfred, the producer and manager of Dr. Feel Good asked.

"This is Miss Pretty Skin!" Answered Dr. Feel Good.

"Is she here to work?" Alfred liked what he seen in Cynthia. Cynthia's phone began vibrating in her purse. She pulled it out and seen that it was Karter Calling.

Sinful Behavior

"Hello!" Cynthia quickly answered.

"Hi beautiful!"

"Don't hi beautiful me, Karter! You haven't answered my calls in two days so continue to do what you've been doing!" Cynthia said with attitude as she listened to Dr. Feel Good and Alfred talk about her like she was a prostitute. Dr. Feel Good even tried to raise up her dress, but she slapped his hand away.

"Cynt! I'm sorry! I've just had a lot on my mind with everything going on!" Karter tried to explain, but then wrinkles spread across his forehead when he heard the voice of two different males in the background saying sexual things.

"Whatever Karter! Worry about Elijah, but I'm bout to get me some celebration sex cause I'm single and free to mingle!" Cynthia knew how to ruffle Karter's feathers.

"What? Where are you at?" Karter was now feeling some type of way.

"At the mansion that you fucked me in front of the crowd of people! About to make me a porn! What do you care?" Cynthia knew that her choice of words would make

Karter express how he really felt. Karter felt his heart drop into his big toe. Jealousy, anger and rage filled his soul all at one time.

"What the fuck do you mean about you finna make a porn! Shawty I swear to god if you don't bring your ass to my house right now, I swear it's over between us!" Karter wasn't aware of the emotion he was showing, but the tone of voice he was using let Cynthia know and feel that he wanted her. Not to mention he made her pussy moist, but she wasn't gonna let it be that easy for Karter.

"No Karter! I'm….!"

"Cynt don't fuckin play with me!" Cynthia smiled.

"Okay, damn! I'm on my way!" She hung up the phone.

"So baby, what's up? You ready to make a movie?" Dr. Feel Good grabbed Cynthia on the ass.

"No, I'm sorry! I have to go home to my man!" Cynthia didn't need any help finding the front door.

Thirty minutes later Cynthia pulled into the parking garage of Karter's condo and parked next to his caddy. She smiled at the thought of the morning Karter gave her a ride

Sinful Behavior

to school in the caddy. When Elijah seen her get dropped off by Karter, he got mad. Cynthia knew Elijah was mad because he didn't have a car. Life is crazy, thought Cynthia as she walked to the elevator.

Knock Knock Knock

The door swung open and Karter grabbed Cynthia by her face, kissing her in the mouth. Cynthia had never been kissed with so much fire and desire in her life. The way Karter was kissing her, there was no way he didn't want her to be his woman. Karter picked Cynthia up, carried her to the couch and laid her down on her back. Without wasting any time, Karter pushed Cynthia's dress up and put his face at her love below. Cynthia's pretty plump pussy stared at Karter as he parted her sealed lips with his fingers.

"Aaaaaahhh Kaarteerrr!" Cynthia moaned when she felt Karter's tongue flick across her clitoris while she peeled her dress off of her body. The way Karter took control of Cynthia as soon as the door opened had her pussy pouring juices onto his tongue.

"You like that baby?" Karter said as he ate.

"Yesss babbyyy, yesss!" Cynthia grabbed ahold of Karter's dreads and started rotating her pelvis in a slow rhythm.

"You taste so good baby!"

"Come fuck me Karter!" Cynthia pulled Karter's head up to her face and stuck her tongue into his mouth tasting her own juices.

"You want this dick baby?" Karter pulled his shorts off.

"Give me my dick! Oooh babbyy!" Cried Cynthia when she felt the fat head of Karter's short dick widen the entrance of her pussy.

"Daaaam baby!" Karter whispered into Cynthia's ear when he felt the extremely hot temperature of her insides. Her pussy walls gripped his dick as he inched all four inches inside of her.

"Kaaaaarteer you feeeel sooo goooood!" Cooed Cynthia as she grabbed Karter by his ass cheeks, pulling him closer and making him give her all. I've never felt anything like this before in my life, thought Karter as he felt the insides of Cynthia's vagina grip the head of his dick, making it pulsate.

Sinful Behavior

"Ummmm yesss daddy fuck meeee!" Cynthia loved the way Karter was delivering short hard pumps inside of her.

"Ahhh shiiit!" Karter locked his ass cheeks and began pumping faster. Cynthia felt an explosion building up inside of her.

"Kaaaaaarrrter I'mm cumminnn!" She cried sending Karter overboard and they came together.

"Huuu, hu, hu, haaa!" Karter nutted inside of Cynthia and collapsed onto her breast. Cynthia ran her fingers through Karter's dreads.

"Baby!" He said breathing heavily.

"Yes baby!" Cynthia looked at Karter as he raised his head to look at her.

"I love you and I wanna spend the rest of my life with you!" Cynthia smiled and her eyes teared up. Karter watched as a trail of tears ran from her eyes.

"Baby what's wrong?" Karter asked as he sat up. Then he wiped her tears away.

"I don't wanna get hurt again!" She admitted.

Michael "Oodoo" Smith

"You have nothing to worry about baby! I put that on Deacon Jones!" Karter wanted Cynthia to know he was telling the truth and she could trust him with her heart.

"What about your boy, Elijah?"

"I'm going to the jail tomorrow to talk to him and let him know everything. I think he'll understand and if not, he'll have no other choice, but to if he doesn't want to spend more time than he has to in jail!" Cynthia raised up. Karter really had her attention now.

"What do you mean if he doesn't wanna stay in there longer than he has to? That lil girl's family has a protection order on him that is preventing him from bonding out!" Karter stood up from off of Cynthia and walked to the kitchen island. He got the note Thomas wrote and he took it to Cynthia.

"Read this Cynt!" Karter handed the note to Cynthia then he went got his phone from the kitchen because it was vibrating. Damn! This is Thomas, thought Karter when he seen the contact name on the screen.

"Thomas! What's up?" Karter said loud enough to make sure Cynthia heard him as he sat next to her and put his phone on speakerphone.

Sinful Behavior

"I don't have the time to talk! Turn the TV on right now to channel 8 news. Right now, Karter! Take care of my nieces!" Thomas hung up.

"Thomas! Thomas!" Cynthia yelled but it was too late. Karter quickly scrambled to get the remote to turn on the TV. When the TV came on and he turned to channel 8 news, him and Cynthia couldn't believe their own eyes. Oh my God, thought Cynthia as she watched Thomas on the news live holding the clerk at the bank at gun point. The negotiator was trying to convince him to put the gun down, but Thomas wasn't hearing nothing he was saying. Cynthia and Karter watched as Thomas pushed the female bank clerk to the side and pointed his gun at the crowd of police.

"Ohh! Cynthia covered her mouth as she watched her uncle get gunned down on TV. Karter turned the TV off and took Cynthia into his arms.

"He went out like he wanted to!" Karter rocked Cynthia.

"I know baby! I read the letter!"

****

"Are you sure, you okay? Leikei asked Tasha as she pulled into the club parking lot to go to work.

Michael "Oodoo" Smith

Yeah girl! I'm fine! Go ahead and make your money! Call me, I'll be up!" Tasha was way more sadder than she sounded.

"Okay bitch, but if you need me, call me!" Leikei hung up the phone and got out of her car to go into the club.

Leikei spoke to Big Paul, the security at the front door, who always flirted with her. Then she went to Ralphy's office. She figured he was gonna be talking shit since she hadn't been to work in a few days. She knocked on the door once, then she twisted the knob. When she stepped into the office Ralphy was sitting in his leather recliner, crying. For some reason he looked slimmer to Leikei than he did most days. What the fuck is wrong with him, thought Leikei as she shut the door.

"What's wrong big bruh?" Leikei asked as she took a seat on the opposite side of the desk from Ralphy. Ralphy looked up at leikei then he pulled the drawer out from his desk. Ralphy grabbed a pill bottle and threw them at Leikei. Leikei examined the pill bottle but she wasn't familiar with the name of the pills.

"I've been taking them muthafuckas for the past two years, lil sis! I'm tired of living this sick ass life of

Sinful Behavior

darkness!" Ralphy said through tears. Leikei had never seen Ralphy emotional and she was still lost to what he was talking about.

"Big bruh, what do you mean you tired of living? What's wrong you sick? What's going on?" Leikei was curious.

"I've got HIV, lil sis! I found out about two years ago!" Ralphy watched Leikei's whole facial expression change. She looked like she had seen a ghost. I fuckin knew it, thought Leikei as she got up from her seat to go give Ralphy a hug. Leikei had overheard one of the girls that used to work at the club cussin Ralphy out one night, callin him all type of sick bitches.

"Damn big bruh, I'm sorry to hear that this is going on with you!" Leikei sat the pills on the desk and wrapped her arms around Ralphy's neck.

"I got mad love for you no matter what big bruh! You've been there for me since day one!" Leikei meant every word.

"I love you too, lil sis! That's why I'm tellin you. I don't want everybody to know my business. The doctor told me as long as I take my medication, I can't give it to nobody, and I've been doin that since I first found out!" Ralphy lied as he wiped his face. Yeah fuckin right thought Leikei.

"I got you bruh! Your business is your business!" Leikei took her arms from around Ralphy's neck. Then she dug in her purse to get the money to pay her tip out.

"Don't worry bout your tip out lil sis! Go get your money and if you lay up with any of them niggas that be comin up in here, you make sure that you make them niggas strap up!"

"Okay big bruh! I got you!" Leikei left out of the office. Damn Tash Tash might have that pack, thought Leikei as she headed for the dressing room.

****

"What's up unc? Mama told me that you wanted me to call you ASAP! What's the emergency?" Big Pokie was using the wall phone inside of D-Block of the Fulton County Jail.

"That punk muthafuckin preacher who tried to rape ya lil cousin is in there somewhere!" Tevin told his nephew Big Pokie who was in the same jail as Elijah.

"Oh yeah! What's the name?"

"Elijah Woods!"

"What he look like?" Big Pokie started looking around the unit.

"Brown skin! Around six-one!"

"Nigga got wavy hair and invisible sets in his mouth?" Big Pokie ran his hand over his goatee.

"Yeah, how you know nephew?"

"Believe it or not, I'm looking at the pretty muthafucka right now! I'll hit you back fam!" Big Pokie hung up the phone and walked three phones down to Elijah, who was on the phone in the middle of a conversation.

"Yeah, baby don't worry yourself, okay!" Elijah told Tasha as he saw a shadow cover the wall he was facing. He turned around to see what it was. A six-five muscular monster was standing only inches from Elijah's face.

"Phone check shawty!" Big Pokie growled as he hung up Elijah's call. Then he smacked the taste out of Elijah's mouth, making blood escape his mouth. Elijah dropped the receiver and tried to regain his balance.

Michael "Oodoo" Smith

"You like raping lil girls, huh?" Big Pokie reached back to punch Elijah in his face, but when he swung his arm got caught. Big Pokie turned to the right and saw that it was his big homie holding his arm by the wrist.

"Act like you wanna buck and I'll break your muthafuckin arm off!" James Jr. was way smaller than Big Pokie, but he was extremely strong and well known for beating a muthafucka into a coma. Thank god, thought Elijah when he seen his big brother.

"OG, he tried to rape my lil cousin!" Big Pokie plead his case.

"You got proof nigga?" James Jr. had the meanest mug anybody ever wanted to see.

"No! I don't OG!" Big Pokie dropped his head knowing that he wasn't ready to go to war with James Jr.

"Okay! Then find you something else to do!" James Jr. threw Big Pokie's arm away from him. Without looking at Elijah, James Jr. walked back to his rack, where he sat down and started back reading his novel "The G In Game." Elijah was so glad that his brother whom he hadn't seen in forever was there to save him. He wiped the blood from his mouth and walked over to James Jr.'s rack.

Sinful Behavior

"Whatchu want?" James Jr. asked Elijah without looking up from his book.

"I, I just wanted to thank you for what you just done!"

"Don't thank me! Thank your daddy! If it was up to me, I would've let the lil homie smash your bitch ass, but I know that daddy would roll over in his grave. So, I let the lil homie do what I wanted to do to you myself before I stopped it!" James Jr. turned the page of his book. Elijah was lost for words. He knew he wasn't worthy of his brother saving him. Elijah knew that he wasn't worthy of his brother saving him. Elijah knew that he had abandoned his family for Pastor Dawson's family. Everything Elijah had did over the past 17 years came colliding in on his heart. His emotions swirled up like a tornado and he couldn't hold back the back the tears as he sat by James Jr.'s feet.

"Bruh, I'm sorry! I know I fucked up! My whole life is fucked up!" Elijah cried, but James Jr. burst into Laughter.

"Hahahah! Have you ever read one of Michael "Oodoo" Smith novels? Dude is a fool wit it!" James Jr. turned the page of his novel paying Elijah no attention.

Michael "Oodoo" Smith

After Elijah drowned in his tears for another three minutes James Jr. sat down his novel.

"Look Shawty! I'm gonna be straight up with you! You's ah fucked up individual. Nigga when was the last time you visited mama? Felicia and Renee have never even met your kids cause you to good to go to Mechanicsville to visit your own fuckin sistas, who stole clothes out of the mall fa ya punkass to be fresh at school. I've been out of prison for five years and this my first time seeing you. You think since you give mama a band to give me when I got home from the chain gang that you something, huh nigga?" James Jr.'s words cut through Elijah's soul like a sword as he listened to the truth be delivered.

"You got a million-dollar crib that ain't a muthafucka in your family been too! Shawty you super fucked up, fake as hell and whatever you going through, you probably deserve it! But who am I to judge you, my baby brotha, the Almighty Pastor Elijah Malikah Woods!" James Jr. picked up his novel. Elijah broke down like someone close to him had died.

"I, I, I fucked up bruh! Ev, ev, everything you said is true! Arrrrghhh!" Elijah screamed releasing the pain

Sinful Behavior

inside of him causing the entire unit to look at him. James Jr. sat his novel down, looked at Elijah and shook his head.

"Come here boy! You still my baby!" James Jr. wrapped his arms around Elijah. After a good tight hug James Jr. let Elijah loose.

"I hope you can see what life is teaching you at this very moment. You can grow rich and abandon the ones that were there for you from the beginning, but when you hit rock bottom somehow nobody will be there for you, but the ones who truly love you! Your family!" James Jr. looked around and seen that everyone was looking at them. He stood up.

"What the fuck ya'll lookin at? Ya'll niggas must want some smoke?" James Jr. loudly announced in the unit causing everybody to start back minding their own business. Then he sat down and opened his box. He took out a new pair of boxers, a rag, a bar of dial soap, a towel, t-shirt, and socks. Then he handed it to Elijah.

"Gone in there and take you a shower. Talk to Jesus while you in there and come back out a new man!" Elijah did as his brother told him to. When he got out of the shower James Jr. had fixed them a jailhouse burrito to eat. They ate and discussed everything that was going on

Michael "Oodoo" Smith

with the two of them. Elijah was dumbfounded when James Jr. mentioned Cynthia and how she sent him money, wrote him and even had went to visit him while he was in the chain gang. Elijah didn't even know that his wife and kids knew his big brother. Elijah quickly realized that he had a good woman that he had mistreated and abused for years just like Pastor Dawson had did her mother.

CHAPTER 9

Elijah Jr.'s pounding headache woke him up out of his sleep. He didn't know if it was the side effect from the hormone pills he was taking or not. He shuffled through his bed covers to find his phone while he wondered if Jason had called him or not. Once he located his phone beneath a pillow, he immediately became angry when he seen that Jason had not called or texted him.

Ugly muthafucka ain't texted me since 8 o'clock last night. What the hell does he got goin on? Thought Elijah Jr. as he got out of bed and slid some skinny jeans over the G-string he was wearing. He gonna wish he would've called when he see this ass in these jeans, thought Elijah Jr. as he tugged at the button on his jeans to snap them close. Then he called Jason's phone, but he didn't receive an answer.

Elijah Jr. grabbed his keys and seven minutes later he pulled into the driveway of Jason's parents' house. Jason was spoiled therefore the two-story guest house that sat in the back of the main house was his all to himself. Jr.

got out of the car and walked into the backyard to the guesthouse. He twist the knob and the door was unlocked so he walked inside. Music was playing upstairs so Elijah Jr. started up the stairs. Damn music so loud, that's why he can't hear his phone ringing, thought Elijah Jr. as he traveled upstairs, but when he reached the top step, he saw exactly why he hadn't heard from the love of his life.

"Ooooh Quinton! Fuck me baby!" Jason screamed loud as the dude behind him dropped dick off in him. Tears flooded Elijah Jr.'s eyes.

Jr. felt as if his world had come to an end. Not being able to watch any longer, he turned around and headed back down the stairs feeling like he had no reason to live. Jr. drove home in a funk state of mind while he cried his heart away. Jason was his everything and for him to be fucking someone else proved to Elijah Jr. that Jason didn't give a rat's ass about him. I don't wanna live anymore, thought Elijah Jr. as he pulled into his driveway. Suicidal thoughts infiltrated his mind as he got out of the car to go into the house, but the car pulling into the driveway captured his attention.

"Who is that Samantha?" Asked Claudia, Samantha's pretty Latin gymnastics coach.

Sinful Behavior

"That's my brother!" Samantha grabbed her gym bag.

"No! He's my husband!" Claudia put her car in park.

"He likes....!" Was all Samantha got to say before Claudia jumped out of the car. Oh well! I guess she'll have to find out in person, thought Samantha as she got out of the car to go into the house.

"Hi handsome!" Claudia said as she walked up to Jr. who was leaning back on his car. Jr.'s heart fluttered, and he felt tingly on the inside. This was the first time he'd ever felt this way from a woman's presence.

"Um, hey!" Jr. froze up causing Claudia to giggle.

"What? Are you shy?" She asked him.

"Um...I don't know, but you are pretty!" He admitted.

"Thanks! I gotta get my other students' home, is there any way I can call you! Maybe we can go out to eat!" Claudia twirled her curly hair.

"Um. Yah! Sure! What's your number?" Jr. pulled out his phone.

Michael "Oodoo" Smith

"404-… …!" Claudia announced her number.

"Okay, I got you!"

"Can I get a hug?" Claudia opened her arms. Jr. smiled then he embraced her, but the feeling in his penis was more intense than sex. Holy shit thought Jr. as he felt his manhood react to a woman's touch.

"Uhmmm! I really needed that! Make sure you call me, handsome!" Claudia let go of Jr. to walk to her car. What the fuck is really going on, thought Samantha as she watched her brother blush as Claudia walked away. Damn I'm glad she pulled up! I was about to blow my brains out, thought Jr. as he waved at Claudia, who was pulling out of the driveway.

****

Tasha woke up early feeling sick. She ran to the toilet and vomited as soon as she got out of the bed. Her stomach was tore up. She ended up taking a number two. She figured it was something she had eaten that had her stomach upset because she'd taken numerous pregnancy tests and they all came back negative. When she finished using the bathroom, she showered then got ready to go visit Elijah at the jail. The tight-fitting Fashion Nova outfit

Sinful Behavior

Tasha put on would've made you think she was on her way to the club. Thirty minutes later she was walking inside of the Fulton County Jail turning the heads of everyone inside the waiting area. This muthafucka looks like she headed to the club, thought Karter when he saw Tasha enter the waiting area.

"Karter Jones!" The CO sitting behind the desk yelled out and Karter got up to go inside the visitation room. Tasha waved at Karter as he walked by. She really has some nerves, thought Karter. He went in the visitation room and sat down at the monitor the CO told him to sit down at. Karter picked up the reciever.

"What's up bruh?" Elijah said smiling when the screen came on, but Karter's facial expression wasn't so happy Gilmore.

"What's up Elijah? Look, bruh, I'm not gonna lie to you or make it sound fly to you! Me and Cynthia have been seeing each other!" At that very moment Elijah's heart tightened up and he got lightheaded. He couldn't believe what his right-hand man was sitting on the screen telling him.

"So that's how y'all do me, huh? Damn bruh, for real!" A tear rolled from Elijah's eyes.

Michael "Oodoo" Smith

"To be honest Elijah, you did it to yourself. But I ain't finna debate about who's right or who's wrong! I got the evidence you need to get your charges dropped on this bullshit case they holding you on. But my question to you is, are we beefing because me and Cynthia are about to be a happy couple!" Karter gave it to Elijah straight up raw. Elijah rubbed his chin then nodded his head up and down, completely awestruck by the news.

"Hmm! So, I guess you're gonna take over the church too, since you taking everything else of mines!" Elijah tried to be sarcastic.

"It's funny that you say that cause the church board has voted for me to take over the pulpit!" Karter told Elijah what he had already knew.

"You deserve it Karter! Hell, it was yours in the first place! The church and Cynthia were yours! I guess I was just holding it down until you became man enough to step up to the plate!" Elijah tried to throw a low blow, but Karter was unaffected.

"I guess so Elijah! I'ma talk to Deyonda so they will take the protection order off you and I'm gonna give Candriah the evidence tape to get your charges dropped!" Karter had nothing else to say. Elijah hated the fact that he had to accept everything that was being thrown at him, which forced him to swallow his pride.

"I'd greatly appreciate that Karter! Thanks!" Elijah somehow managed to say.

"No problem!" Karter hung up the receiver, stood up and walked away from the screen. Look at her triflin ass, thought Karter as he passed Tasha on his way out of the visitation monitor room.

Tasha sat down at the monitor and picked up the phone. The look on Elijah's face told Tasha that he was in a foul mood.

"What's wrong baby? You look like you are not happy to see me!" The look on Elijah's face was making Tasha tear up. Elijah dropped his head and shook it. Then he looked back up at Tasha.

"No Tasha! I'm good! I should be out very soon! I'm all yours! Karter just told me that him and Cynthia are in a relationship!" Tasha's mouth gaped open.

"I knew he wasn't your real friend, baby! They probably been fuckin around since they were teenagers! Fuck them baby! I'm all you need!" Tasha was so happy on the inside.

Tasha felt awesome when she left from visiting with Elijah. When she pulled into her mother's driveway, she became confused when she seen twenty big ass U-Haul boxes stacked up in the front yard. Tasha got out of the car and walked up to the boxes.

"Elijah's belongings!" Tasha read the labels on the boxes.

****

Elijah went back to his unit feeling bad that he was about to lose everything, but he was glad that he was about to get out of jail. James Jr. hung up the wall phone and went to his rack smiling. What is he so happy about, thought Elijah as he sat down on his rack that was next to James Jr.'s.

"What's up Shawty? Did you hear some good news?" James Jr. asked Elijah who looked confused.

"Bruh, I've lost my wife to my best friend and I've lost my church!" Elijah shook his head.

"I done already heard Shawty! I just got off da phone wit my sis, Cynthia! She about to come pay off my restitution and get me out. She told me about her new dude Karter! He was supposed to hook me up with a job at the

Sinful Behavior

Benz Dealership, washing cars when I get out! Sis said you should be out either today or tomorrow, so you good!" James Jr. patted his lil brother on the back. Elijah was sick.

"Lil bruh, it ain't too late for you to gain back everything that you've lost and more!" James Jr. tried to motivate Elijah.

"Inmate James Woods Jr. ATW!" The CO announced over the intercom. James Jr. jumped up.

"Cynthia came quick as hell! Hey bruh you can have all that shit in that box, I'm out!" James Jr. was too happy to be leaving. Elijah stood up.

"I'll call you as soon as I get out, bruh!" Said Elijah.

"Don't worry bout me! I know Shawty Shawty gonna keep her word! You don't be in here worried either! Just be happy and know that your situation could be worse!" With that said James Jr. grabbed his mat and went to the door to leave, leaving his baby bruhda behind. So be happy cause my situation could be worse, tuah! Yeah, right, thought Elijah as he watched his brother leave.

With his brother gone Elijah had nobody there to protect him and make him feel safe. After about a hour after James Jr. left, anxiety set in on Elijah and he began thinking about all of his problems. He needed to talk to someone, so he decided to call Tasha.

"Hey baby!" Tasha excitedly accepted Elijah's call.

"I just want you to know that I've lost everything from my wife to my church, all to Karter and it's all your fault!" Elijah blamed Tasha. He had came to his senses and he realized she was the root of all of his problems.

"So, you really gonna call me and blame me for your fuck ups! Nigga you was the one chasing me, but don't worry, I'll get the money for an abortion!" Tasha knew Elijah was gonna be lost when she mentioned an abortion.

"Huh? What do you mean an abortion?" Elijah's whole tone of voice changed.

"I'm fuckin pregnant and you callin me wit some bullshit! Fuck you Elijah!" Tasha's voice was crackin.

"Baby wait!"

"I'm tired of you hurtin my feelins for no reason!" Cried Tasha. Then she hung up.

Sinful Behavior

"Baby! Baby!" Elijah knew she'd hung up when he heard the dial tone. He tried calling her back several times, but she didn't answer. Elijah went and sat on his rack, hoping that Tasha was pregnant with a boy since his other son was gay.

****

Karter had been running around since he opened his eyes. After he dropped the bomb on Elijah, he went ahead and lined James Jr. up with the job at the dealership as soon as he got out of jail. While he was in the process of getting James Jr. the job Karter realized that he should open his own detail shop and he went to look at a building that he found online while James Jr. was getting interviewed.

Karter and Cynthia made plans to go to dinner at 8 o'clock. I got the taste for some shrimp, thought Karter as he turned off the shower. He couldn't wait to tell Cynthia that he had already got James Jr. a job. He stepped out of the shower and grabbed his towel. After he wrapped the towel around his waist, he picked up his phone to see what time it was. 6:15! That's perfect timing, he thought as he headed into his room.

ZZZZZ ZZZZ ZZZZ

His phone vibrated in his hand. Karter looked at the screen as he sat down on the edge of his bed. What does she want, thought Karter when he seen that it was Tasha calling him using Facebook.

"Yeah!" Karter put his phone on speakerphone so he could dry off.

"I'm not interrupting anything, am I?" Tasha spoke softly into the phone.

"No! You good! What's up?"

"I don't know if you've talked to your homeboy or not, but this morning after I left from seeing him, he called me accusing me and you for him losing everything!" Tasha started crying.

"I can't do this Karter! I'm just gonna kill myself! I'm tired of being the blame!" Cried Tasha.

"Whoa, whoa, whoa! Tasha hold up! Don't talk like that!" Karter heard the seriousness in Tasha's voice, so he tried to calm her down.

"No! It's over! I don't wanna live anymore!" Tasha screamed convincingly.

Sinful Behavior

"No Tasha! Listen! Where are you?" Karter picked up his phone. He couldn't let Tasha hurt herself.

"' At home!"

"What's your address?"

"For what? So, you can send somebody over here! I don't want to talk to anybody!" Tasha screamed into the phone. This bitch is crazy, thought Karter.

"I promise I'll be alone! Just send me the address!"

"Karter, I swear if you bring or send anybody else, I'll blow my brains out by the time they knock at my door!" Karter believed that Tasha meant business.

"Tasha! Just chill! Please message me your address! I'm on my way right now!" Said Karter as he slid into a pair of Jordan sweatpants and t-shirt instead of the outfit he had planned on wearing to dinner with Cynthia. When Tasha didn't respond Karter looked at his phone and a message came through on Messenger. It was Tasha's address.

****
*

I got time to get me some dick, thought Cynthia as she got off of I-20 West to surprisingly show up at Karter's condo while she called his phone to make sure that he was at home.

"Hello!" Karter sounded bothered when he answered the phone.

"Hey baby! What's up?" Cynthia noticed the odd tone of voice from Karter.

"Nothin! Hey Cynt, something came up, so we'll have to have dinner tomorrow! Okay baby!" Karter put his caddy in reverse to leave out of the parking deck.

"Um, okay! Is everything okay?" Cynthia was concerned.

"Yeah! I mean, I hope so! I'll call you back later!" Karter hung up on Cynthia, leaving her feeling some type of way.

As soon as Cynthia sat her phone in her lap, she seen Karter driving out of the parking deck. I wonder where he is going that is so important that he cancelled our dinner date and hung up on me, thought Cynthia as she watched Karter get in traffic.

Sinful Behavior

"The only way to find out is to see!" Cynthia said out loud as she got in the turning lane to follow Karter. For 13 minutes Cynthia stayed five car lengths behind Karter's caddy until he pulled into the parking deck of Sky Rise Condos. Who lives here, thought Cynthia. Then she remembered where she had seen the name of the condos at. This is where Elijah bought a condo for that girl at, thought Cynthia as she turned into the parking deck behind a Pizza Hut delivery man and crept around slowly until she could see Karter's caddy without him seeing her. The delivery guy's car provided Cynthia with enough shelter to not be seen by Karter as he got out of the car.

Cynthia's feelings became numb when she seen Elijah's Benz truck parked next to a car he'd bought for Tasha. I wonder if this place is in Elijah's name, thought Cynthia as she watched Karter get into the elevator. The pizza delivery guy got out of his car and started towards the elevator. Cynthia quickly got out of her car and ran up to the elevator.

"Hey! Excuse me!" Cynthia got the delivery man's attention while they waited for the elevator.

"Yes ma'am! How can I help you!" He asked her.

"I just moved over here, and I wanted to make sure that this address was coming up in your computer when I give you my number! This is for your time!" Cynthia handed the young black delivery guy a fifty-dollar bill as they stepped onto the elevator.

"Um, sure! What's your number!" He asked Cynthia. She gave him Elijah's phone number and sure enough it came back to 1400 Sky Rise Condos, door number 4A.

****

Ring Ding Dong

Karter rang the doorbell of door 4A. A minute later the door came open and Karter was lost for words. Tasha stood in front of him as naked as the day she was born. I see why that nigga done lost his mind, thought Karter as he forgot the real reason that he had come to Tasha's house.

"What's wrong Karter? Cat got your tongue!" Tasha said seductively as she ran her hand ova her pretty pussy cat. What the fuck, thought Tasha when she seen who appeared behind Karter.

Sinful Behavior

"Karter why are you just poppin up at my house! Elijah is not here!" Tasha quickly flipped the script on Karter.

"Huh? What?" Karter twisted his face in confusion.

"Yeah, Karter! What are you doing?" Karter heard a very familiar voice behind him say. No fuckin way thought Karter as he slowly turned around to find Cynthia standing right behind him.

"You need to leave before I call the police on you, Deacon Jones!" Tasha slammed the door, leaving Cynthia and Karter in the hallway. Tasha damn near died laughing.

"Cynt! It's not what you think!" Karter tried to explain.

"You are so right, Karter! Cause it ain't nothin between you and me!" Cynthia turned to leave.

"Baby wait!" Karter grabbed Cynthia's arm.

"Don't fuckin touch me!" Cynthia snatched away from Karter and left even more hurt than she was when she found out that Elijah didn't love her anymore.

Michael "Oodoo" Smith

"Mane! I swear this some Class A bullshiiiit!" Karter couldn't believe how Tasha had just played him like he showed up unannounced at her spot. He knew that he was dead with Cynthia.

Knock Knock Knock

He banged on Tasha's door, but she didn't answer.

"Fuck!" Karter screamed, knowing that Cynthia was through with him forever if he couldn't persuade Tasha to admit the truth to her. He called Cynthia's phone as he walked to the elevator, but he quickly realized that he was on bocklist.

****

"Niggas ain't shit!" Cynthia screamed as she slapped the steering wheel with her hand. Cynthia was torn on the inside. Why can't I have a real man that will keep it real with me no matter what, thought Cynthia as she looked down to grab her vibrating phone from off her lap.

"Hello!" She answered with an attitude.

"Shawty Shawty!" James Jr.'s voice always made Cynthia smile.

Sinful Behavior

"Hey Shawty Shawty!" Cynthia smirked through her tears.

"What's wrong baby girl?' James Jr. could tell that something wasn't right with Cynthia.

"It's nothin!" Said Cynthia, but she broke down crying.

"Shawty Shawty! Stop crying and come on over here to Renee's house to kick it with us! She throwing me a fish fry!" Cynthia could hear the music and people in the background.

"Shawty Shawty, I really shouldn't!"

"Woman get over that bullshit and get yo ass ova here! Do you remember where she live?" James Jr. wasn't taking no for an answer.

"Of course, I remember!" Cynthia dried her face.

"Well come on! I need a partna to play Spades with!"

"Okay Shawty Shawty! I'm on my way!" Cynthia hung up the phone. She stopped by the first liquor store that she seen before she made it to Mechanicsville and bought five bottles of Jose Quervo and Cîroc.

Michael "Oodoo" Smith

CHAPTER 10

"Elijah Wood! ATW!" Elijah heard come over the intercom as he watched the news. From the few days he'd been in jail Elijah quickly learned that ATW means "All The Way "meaning that you're going home. Elijah quickly jumped up from where he was sitting and went to grab his mat.

"Hey, young blood! What you gonna do with that commissary in your box?" The older man who slept next to Elijah asked him.

"God bless you! It's all yours!" Elijah grabbed his mat and practically ran to the door. The door popped open and the CO told Elijah to step out. The CO escorted Elijah to the front of the jail, where he got dressed out in his clothes that he wore to jail. After Elijah dressed out the intake and discharge CO gave him his property. Elijah was so happy when he walked through the exit door and seen his lawyer, Candriah waiting for him.

Sinful Behavior

"Your homeboy brought me the tape yesterday and I took it to the prosecutor's office. This morning the DA demanded for all charges against you to be dropped and that you get released from jail immediately!" Candriah smiled.

"That's a blessing! Thanks so much! Can you give me a ride home!" Elijah wanted to surprise Tasha.

"Sure thing! Let's go!"

When Elijah stepped outside of the jail, the aroma of fresh air revitalized his soul. He had never appreciated the sun shining like he did at the very moment. The ride to his condo was quiet. Elijah had three things on his mind. That was to take a shit, shower and go see his sisters.

"Thanks a lot Can Can!"

"I'm just doing my job!" Candriah turned into the parking garage of Sky Rise Condos.

"What the fuck?" Elijah spat out loud when Candriah stopped for him to get out of the car.

"There's your homeboy! Is everything okay?" Candriah asked when she seen Karter walk pass her car. Karter had made her promise to text him when Elijah was getting released if she wanted the evidence to get Elijah out and she held up her part of the bargain.

"Yeah! Yeah! Everything's good!" Elijah watched Karter push the button on the elevator.

"Thanks again!" Elijah jumped out of the car in a hurry to catch Karter.

"Aye! Karter!" Elijah screamed getting Karter's attention as he got ready to get onto the elevator.

"What's up!" Karter calmly asked Elijah as he held the elevator door open for him.

"What are you doing over here?" Elijah asked as he watched Karter press four on the button for the floors. Karter looked up at Elijah and shook his head.

"Man, I had no idea that she was gonna have me and you over here at the same time!" Karter unlocked his phone.

"What? Who?" Elijah couldn't believe his ears. If she did this I'm done with her ass and I mean that, thought Elijah.

"Tasha wild ass hell! Look! She hit me up on Facebook tellin me that she wanna fuck and eat my ass.

Sinful Behavior

Then she sent me the address, so I came over here! She said y'all wasn't together anymore cause you called her blaming her for everything that has happened!" Karter showed Elijah where Tasha had called and sent the address. Elijah's heart rate sped up and a midst of sweat appeared on his nose. He was speechless.

Ding

The elevator opened.

"She does live in 4A, doesn't she?" Karter asked.

"Yeah, come on!" Elijah led the way to condo 4A. Elijah was so mad that he knocked on the door instead of ringing the doorbell.

Knock Knock Knock

Tasha got up out of the bed to go see who was knocking on her door. Somebody at the wrong door, thought Tasha as she made her way to the door.

"Baby!" Tasha screamed in excitement when she looked through the peephole and saw Elijah.

"Baby!" Tasha snatched the door open, but she quickly stopped screaming when she seen Karter standing behind Elijah smiling.

"So, you wanna fuck Karter and eat his ass you stupid bitch!" Elijah yelled with a menacing mug on his face.

"Baby he's lying!" Tasha tried to explain as Elijah stormed past her.

"He ain't lying! He showed me the messages! Get your shit and get the fuck out!" Elijah had taken all he could take. Karter was shocked. He had never seen Elijah like this. Got damn about time nigga, thought Karter, happy that Elijah was handling Tasha like the hoe that she was.

"So, you gonna believe this nigga who went behind your back and fucked your wife, over me, your child's mother! You know what, you'll never see this child! You son of a bitch! Y'all can go have ménage trois with your wife for all I give a fuck!" With no shoes on her feet wearing only a T-shirt, Tasha grabbed her keys off the counter to leave. But before she could grab her purse, Elijah grabbed her arm.

"So, you gonna keep my baby away from me!" Elijah's whole demeanor changed. This nigga is a real sucka, thought Karter as he watched the soap opera in front of him.

Sinful Behavior

"You treatin me like I'm nothin! All I've done is be good to you!" Tasha started crying. Elijah tried to hug her, but she pushed him off of her.

"Get the fuck off me!" She yelled.

"Baby, I'm sorry! You know I've been through so much these past few days!" Elijah apologized as he wrapped his arms around Tasha. Look at this cheese puff ass nigga, thought Karter and he left.

Wheew! That was close! Bitch ass nigga had my baby ready to kick me out, thought Tasha as she watched Karter walk away from the door while she rested her head on Elijah's shoulder.

Sniff Sniff

"I'm sorry baby!" Elijah said when he heard Tasha sniffling.

"You know that there's all type of Apps and shit people can use to make up stuff on their phones!" Tasha stepped back and wiped the tears from her face.

"I know baby! I apologize!" Elijah got down on his knee and raised up Tasha's T-shirt. He kissed her stomach while Tasha rubbed the top of his head.

Michael "Oodoo" Smith

"You stink!" Tasha could smell the jailhouse scent coming from Elijah. She hated the way the jail smelled. She had to stay in jail for a week when she lived in Miami.

"I know right! I'm about to shower because I got somewhere to go that I should've been went to years ago!" Elijah stood up and kissed Tasha on her lips. Then he went to go shower. Damn! I guess we won't be fuckin, thought Tasha as she trailed Elijah's path.

Elijah got out of the shower and got dressed in a navy blue and white Balmain outfit with the matching number six Jordan's to go with it. Where the fuck is, he going, thought Tasha as she watched Elijah spray himself with some Creed cologne.

"Where are you going baby?" She asked.

"To my sister Renee's house!"

"So, you just gonna leave me here?" Tasha said with a slight attitude.

"Of course, not beautiful! Throw on some clothes so we can be on our way!"

Sinful Behavior

"I'm ready!" Tasha threw the bed covers off of her and jumped out of the bed fully dressed, ready to go. All she had to do was throw on her heels.

"Come on, crazy!" Elijah laughed.

(Music Playing)

'Never would've made it

Never could've made it, without you

I would've lost it all, but now I see

How you were there for me

I can sing

Never would've made it

Never could've made it, without you

I would've lost it all, but now I see

How you were there for me

I can sing

I'm stronger

I'm wiser

I'm better

Michael "Oodoo" Smith

Much better

When I look back

Overall you brought me through

I can see that you

Are the one I hold onto

The sounds of Marvin Sapp flowed from the speakers of Elijah's GLE Benz truck while he drove to his sister's house. For some reason the song had more substance to it than it did before to Elijah.

"Baby, do we have to listen to this right now?" Tasha wasn't trying to listen to gospel music at the moment.

"You can change it baby!" Elijah permitted Tasha to do as she pleased as he always did with her. She quickly hooked her phone into the USB cord to play some music off her playlist.

(Music Playing)

'Don't ask no questions

Jus rub my shouldas

When I'm unda pressure

Sinful Behavior

I'm doing what

Your last nigga could neva

Fuck up the store

Blow a bag when I'm with her

  What ever

  You want you can get it

  Ain't wit no extra shit

  She bout ha chedda

  Love when I smile

  She say it make ha wetta

  My ride or die

  She told me it's whatever!'

Tasha recited Moneybagg Yo's song "Wateva I'm wit" word for word as soon as it came on. She even made hand motions to express how she was feeling the lyrics. Elijah smiled, feeling that Tasha was singing to him. All of her antics and actions were foreign to Elijah and he liked it.

Michael "Oodoo" Smith

When Elijah pulled in front of Renee's house in Mechanicsville, the grill was smoking and there was people on the porch smoking, drinking and playing dominoes. Is this the right address, thought Elijah as he put his truck in park. Then he saw James Jr. come out of the front door holding a pan of seasoned meat to put on the grill. Elijah looked over at Tasha, who didn't seem to be bothered by the scenery in front of her.

"Come on baby!" Elijah killed the motor then he opened his door and stepped out of the truck squinching his face from the sunlight beaming in his eyes. Tasha followed Elijah's lead. Elijah quickly realized that he didn't know one person on the porch except for his brother. Two lil boys on scooter bikes rolled up on Elijah forcing him to move his feet so that they didn't run over his shoes.

"Give me five dollars!" The little boy with the Nappy Nation haircut told Elijah.

"I want five dollars too!" Said the other little boy with the dreads in his head.

"Y'all don't even know me and you just rolled up on me demanding money!" Elijah said with a smile, but the six-year-old with Nappy Nation didn't find anything funny.

Sinful Behavior

"I said give me five dollars!" Lil Nappy Nation pulled a gun from beneath his shirt. Elijah's heart skipped a beat and Tasha jumped behind him for protection.

"Bruh!" Elijah wave over James Jr.

"What's up Shawty?"

"Y'all just letting the kids run around with guns!" Elijah was spooked. James Jr. started laughing.

"Hahahahah! Shawty, you really need to start comin to da hood more often! That's a fake gun! Montez this your uncle Elijah!" James Jr. told Lil Nappy Nation who had the gun in his hand.

"That's all he had to say! But I still want my five dollars!" Montez tucked away his fake gun.

"Whose son, is he?" Elijah wanted to know.

"He's Renee's baby boy! Gone in the house! She would love to see you! What has it been, ten years!" James Jr. walked back to the grill. Elijah looked down and the two lil boys were standing there with their hands out.

"Wow! I'm getting jacked by my nephews!" Elijah pulled out his money clip.

"Just look at it like you made an investment! You never know, we might grow up to be something one day!" Montez smiled as he grabbed the money from Elijah.

"Who is that guy baby?" I think I've seen him somewhere before, thought Tasha as they walked up on the porch.

"My big brother! James Jr.!" Said Elijah as he observed the cold stares of the people sitting on the porch. He opened the front door and walked in.

"Renee!" Elijah yelled, standing by the front door.

"Yeah!" He heard someone yell from up the hall, so he started into the house with Tasha on his heels, but after a few steps Elijah saw people sittin in the living room smoking and playing cards, so he stopped walking.

"You lookin like you lost or something!" Renee said as she walked down the hallway towards Elijah.

"Nah sis! I....!" Elijah's words got caught in his throat when he realized who the person was with a towel wrapped around her head, walking behind Renee. Renee looked back to see what Elijah was looking at.

Sinful Behavior

"What you lookin at ha fa? Shawty Shawty been over here chilin wit da fam since last night! Who is this you got wit you!" Renee asked Elijah as she hugged him. He kept his eyes glued to Cynthia who went and sat on the floor in front of the couch.

"My girl, Tasha!" He answered. Damn! Cynthia really over here like she belongs here. Where is her car though? What is she doing smoking weed, thought Elijah as he watched Cynthia hit a J-baby.

"Nice to meet you, girl! Y'all make yaselves at home! I gotta put these braids in Shawty Shawty's hair!" Renee went and sat behind Cynthia.

"Cynthia, what are you doing smoking that stuff?" Elijah couldn't hold his tongue any longer. Ain't he concerned about the wrong bitch, thought Tasha as she took a seat in an empty chair right next to where her and Elijah was standing. Cynthia looked up at Elijah and she took a long drag from the joint between her lips.

"Boy, don't come ova here tryin ta start nothin wit Shawty Shawty and you got a whole notha women wit you!" Renee grabbed the joint from Cynthia. Elijah was about to say something, but the front door came open, grabbing his attention.

Michael "Oodoo" Smith

"Aunty, that muthafucka ride like a real space shuttle!" Lil Dunn Dunn, Renee's second to oldest son walked pass Elijah to hand Cynthia her keys. She even let this nigga drive her car, thought Elijah. Oh shit, thought Tasha, hoping Dunn Dunn didn't remember her face.

"Dunothan! So, I guess you grown now!" Elijah couldn't believe how much his nephew had grown up. Dunn Dunn turned around, looking Elijah up and down. He had no respect for Elijah.

"It's Dunn Dunn to you nigga!" Dunn Dunn was trained to go and there was no exception for Elijah. Elijah smirked.

"And when you became Dunn Dunn?" Like you a somebody thought Elijah. Dunn Dunn turned his head to the left and noticed Tasha.

"Tuah! Fake ass preacher!" Dunn Dunn waved off Elijah and turned to Tasha. Fuck, thought Tasha knowing that Dunn Dunn knew who she was.

"Damn baby, where you been? Ain seen you since I stopped fuckin with Leikei!" Tasha squinched her face and shook her head no like she didn't know what Dunn Dunn was talking about.

Sinful Behavior

"You don't know her!" Elijah spoke up when he seen that Tasha looked uncomfortable.

"Mama, you better tell ya lil brother who Dunn Dunn is!" Dunn Dunn pulled out his phone and went to his media files. Then he pressed play and passed the phone to his mama. Renee looked at his phone and laughed. Then she started the video over and passed the phone to Cynthia who looked at the short video clip of Leikei and Tasha getting fucked by several dudes in what appeared to be a Trap House. Tasha had no idea what they were looking at, but she was ready to go.

"I'm ready to go!" Tasha stood up and pulled on Elijah.

"I know you is!" Said Renee. Her and Cynthia burst into laughter as Cynthia handed Dunn Dunn his phone.

"Preacher man, you ain't gots yaself nothin!" Dunn Dunn found the other video and gave Elijah his phone. Elijah pressed play and Tasha was eating Leikei's pussy while they were surrounded by numerous dicks. Tasha ran out of the front door crying. What the fuck, thought Elijah in total embarrassment.

Michael "Oodoo" Smith

"Don't worry Preacher man! That was on my birthday last year! Now you see why they call me, Dunn Dunn!" Dunn Dunn laughed, and James Jr. came through the front door.

"What's goin on in here?" Asked James Jr. He had seen Tasha run pass him crying.

"Preacher man dun come ova here wit dat stripper prostitute, like she tha best thang smokin!" Dunn Dunn had everybody laughing. Elijah dropped tha phone and ran out of the house after Tasha.

"What the fuck dat bitch done did to baby boi to have him runnin behind ha?" James Jr. asked out loud.

"Bitch bout ate his ass! You know that's what them freaked out bitches do to try to hook a nigga dese days!" Renee spoke from experience.

"Damn! I heard that the Voodoo is in the DooDoo!" James Jr. made everybody laugh.

Elijah got in his truck unphased about what he had seen on the video. He pulled up on Tasha and rolled down the window.

Sinful Behavior

"Baby! Tasha!" Elijah screamed out of the window from the truck as Tasha kept walking down the sidewalk crying. She wouldn't even look at Elijah. He parked on the curb and jumped out. He ran up to Tasha and grabbed her by the arm.

"Get off me!" Tasha screamed while she tried to snatch away from Elijah, but he was too strong.

"Baby Chill out!" Elijah grabbed Tasha forcing her to comply with him.

"Fuck you! You chill out! You been back there doggin me out with ya family and ya wife!" Screamed Tasha as she tried to pray away from Elijah.

"Shut the fuck up! That shit was before me! Fuck them! I don't need nobody, but you and my baby!" Elijah growled while he shook Tasha by her shoulders, looking her in her eyes.

"So, you not mad at me?" Tasha asked with a sad puppy face.

"No baby! I love you!" Elijah kissed Tasha on her dick suckers to show her that he wasn't mad.

Michael "Oodoo" Smith

"Now get in the car, so we can go home!" Elijah put his arms around Tasha's neck and guided her to the passenger side of his truck.

This nigga has to really fuckin love me, cause ain't no fuckin way in the hell I would've chased his ass down if the shoe was on the other foot. I gotta hurry up and get pregnant before he finds out that I'm lyin, thought Tasha as she looked at Elijah while he drove. As soon as they made it home, Tasha didn't waste a second before she tore into Elijah, eating him alive. She made sure Elijah was buried deep in womb every time he came.

****

Samantha and Elijah Jr. came to Renee's house right after Elijah left to bring their mother some clothes to put on and her makeup kit. After they spoke to all their family and got some food to go, they left. Cynthia showered and got dressed when Renee got done doing her box braids. I really enjoy being around real people who aren't faking to be something that they aren't, thought Cynthia as she applied her makeup in Renee's room. Renee may have not lived in the best community, but her house was clean, and she made Cynthia feel right at home at all times.

Sinful Behavior

If I drink too many Panty Droppa's, I might end up spending the night again, thought Cynthia as she applied her lip gloss. Pleased with her appearance, Cynthia left out of the bedroom and went to the front where everyone was at.

"Hey! Shawty Shawty! Come here! I got somebody I want you to meet!" James Jr. waved Cynthia over to where he was standing in the kitchen.

Oh lord, who is this Shawty Shawty trying to introduce me to, like he Chuck Daley or some damn body, thought Cynthia as she approached James Jr. who was standing beside some dude, who's back was to her, denying her any visibility of his face.

"What's up Shawty Shawty?" Cynthia asked with a smile as she examined the waves in the man's hair standing with his back to her.

"I want you to meet my boss!" James Jr. smiled.

"Shawty Shawty! You ain't got no damn job!" Cynthia laughed. The man next to James Jr. turned around.

"Yes, he does! He over the detail department at the dealership until we open our own business in a few months!" Karter said with a smile. Cynthia was lost for words.

"I'ma leave yall two to talk! Here Shawty Shawty!" James Jr. handed Cynthia the Panty Droppa that he'd just made for her then he walked to the den.

"What? Tasha's man got out, so she kicked you to the curb!" Cynthia rolled her eyes at Karter then she sipped from her cup through a straw. Karter knew he had that coming from Cynthia.

Cynt! I swear on my father's grave that I wasn't going over there to do anything sexual with that girl!" Pleaded Karter.

"Don't lie on your father! Let him rest in peace!" Cynthia said calmly. Her nonchalant attitude irked Karter's nerves.

"Baby, I fucked up for even going to try to save that bitch from killing herself!" He explained.

"Oh! So, you fell for that one! Tuah!" Cynthia smirked. Damn bay look good with his haircut, thought Cynthia appreciating how handsome Karter was.

Sinful Behavior

"Baby please forgive me! Please Cynt!" Karter begged, but Cynthia didn't respond. She began slightly moving her body to the music playing.

(Music Playing)

'You said you'd never leave me

I said I'll never leave you

But fairy tales don't always come true

You promised to stay with me

I promised to stay with you

I guess you knew and blew a good thing

Babyyy

Cause I'm saying Bye Bye

"Fairy tales don't always come true Karter!" Cynthia snapped her fingers and did a little two step.

"Cynt, baby I'm truly sorry!" Karter grabbed Cynthia by her waist.

"No, you're not!"

"Yes, I am!"

"Shut up Karter and dance with me! Shawty Shawty start that over for me!" Cynthia was feeling herself. Her and Karter danced for the next few songs.

"I see ya Shawty Shawty!" James Jr. said loud and country when he came in the kitchen. Cynthia stepped back and playfully hit James Jr.

"Thanks, bruh! I really needed this time over here with some real folks!" Cynthia loved the love that she received from Elijah's family.

"Shawty Shawty! You are family no matter what! Karter is a good nigga too! If he wasn't I damn sure wouldn't be vouching for him!" James Jr. dapped up Karter.

"I really appreciate that big bruh! I almost lost my baby!" Karter wrapped his arms around Cynthia's neck, but she quickly spinned out of his arms.

"Tuah! Who said that we was together! Shawty Shawty fix me another drink!" They all laughed.

"Ya'll women something serious Shawty Shawty!" James Jr. said before he fixed Cynthia another Panty Droppa.

Sinful Behavior

Michael "Oodoo" Smith

CHAPTER 11

In eight months, Elijah and Cynthia's divorce was finalized. Cynthia was more reasonable than Elijah had ever imagined that she would be. She let him keep his church and one-fourth of the money in their joint bank account. She didn't even ask for child support from him.

Luckily for Elijah his church family forgave him for his infidelities with Tasha, whom of course is his new companion. The false accusations about him trying to rape the young girl is what really saved his face with sixty percent of his congregation. The other forty percent of his congregation didn't forgive him, and they found themselves a new church home. Elijah was seeing a major decrease in the amount of money that was being offered in church. But for the most part Pastor Woods wasn't trippin because he knew with his new podcast, he would have the forty percent that he lost back, plus more.

Sinful Behavior

Tasha hadn't talked to Leikei since Elijah was in jail. She had cut off everybody from her past life and now she was a new wholesome Tasha soon to be Woods that was the perfect angel, seven days out of the week. All she did was shop, especially since she was eight months pregnant with the baby boy that Elijah wanted so bad. To prevent anything from getting in her way, she deleted all of her old social media and changed her number.

"Baby, I don't feel good!" Tasha told Elijah as she raised her head up from his lap while they lay on the couch, watching old episodes of Power. Out of the blue she started having hot flashes.

"What's wrong baby?" Elijah instantly became concerned.

"I don't ewhhhha!" Tasha threw up on the floor in front of the couch and she broke out into cold sweats.

"Damn baby!" Elijah jumped up from the couch and ran to get a bag for her to vomit in. As soon as he handed her the bag, she threw up again and again. Elijah called her doctor to find out what they needed to do.

"This is Dr. John Tomes II and I'm currently on vacation!" Damn thought Elijah as he hung up the phone.

Michael "Oodoo" Smith

"Baby we need to get you to the hospital!" Elijah suggested as he watched Tasha try to catch her breath.

"Umhuu!" Tasha shook her head yes. She felt horrible. This was the first time she had been sick throughout her entire pregnancy. She knew that something had to be wrong for her to start feeling the way she was, out of nowhere.

"I'm finna get you something to put on!" Elijah left Tasha's side to go to their bedroom to get her something warm to put on. The cold February weather was nothing to play with. People all over the south were dying from the flu and pneumonia.

Elijah helped Tasha get dressed and then he took her to the nearest hospital, which was South Fulton Hospital. Cynthia was always sick when she was pregnant with Jr. and Samantha, so this wasn't new to Elijah, but it had been a long time ago. As soon as Elijah parked at the hospital, Tasha told him that she was okay, but he insisted that she be seen by a doctor to make sure that everything was okay. They signed in at the receptionist's desk then they waited for Tasha's name to be called. Twenty-five minutes later Tasha's name was called, and a nurse escorted them to the back, where Tasha started vomiting as soon as she sat down. When the doctor made it to the room she was still throwing up.

"I'm gonna do some blood work on her and give her something for nausea, but she will have to stay here in the room for at least 72 hours until her blood work comes back from the lab!" Doctor Watkins told Elijah.

"Do what you gotta do Doc!" Elijah shook Dr. Watkins hand. Then Dr. Watkins left.

"I don't wanna be in this place baby! The food is horrible!" Said Tasha as soon as the doctor left.

"You don't have any other choice baby!" Elijah kissed Tasha on her forehead. The nurse came in and took Tasha's blood. She also gave her some pills for the nausea. Next, they gave Tasha a room for her stay at the hospital.

****

"Baby why did you get us a room to stay in tonight?" Karter asked Cynthia as they stepped on the elevator of the W downtown.

"Because it's your birthday and I wanted to get us a suite to stay in!" Cynthia said smiling. Her and Karter had been together for a few months and she was confident that she had his undivided attention.

Ding

"Wow! Penthouse Suite, I see!" Karter noticed what floor the elevator stopped on.

"Only the best for you baby!" Cynthia smiled. She was tipsy from all of the shots of Patron she had drank at their dinner. When they made it to their suite, Cynthia slid the card into the door, and they entered the room.

"Heyy! What the fuck!" Karter smiled.

"Happy Birthday baby! I want you to enjoy yourself tonight!" Cynthia knew Karter couldn't believe his eyes by the expression on his face as two naked ebony goddesses got out of the bed and approached him.

"Hi birthday boy! I'm Honey!"

"And I'm Fantasy!" The women introduced themselves. Karter shook his head and looked at Cynthia.

"What?" She asked, but he turned back to the women.

"I really appreciate ya'll comin here, but I got everything I need and more than I can handle, right here

Sinful Behavior

with my fiancé!" Karter pulled out his wallet and gave the women $200 each.

"Here's for your troubles!" Said Karter as he handed them the money. Cynthia couldn't believe that there was a man on earth who would've done what Karter had just done.

"Girl, you got a good muthafuckin man!" Honey told Cynthia.

"I swear you do!" Fantasy added.

"I know right!" Cynthia was shocked. She had never been with a woman, but she was for damn sure thinking about joining Karter with the women she had hired because they were gorgeous.

"I'll be back baby! Do you need anything?" Karter was about to go to the bar until the strippers were gone.

"No baby! I'm good!" Cynthia noticed that Karter didn't look at the two women before he left. She knew then that Karter was the least bit concerned about another woman.

I gotta be the stupidest nigga alive or I just really love Cynthia! Was that some type of test? You just love her, thought Karter as he rode the elevator down to the first floor. He went to the bar and ordered himself a drink. As soon as he downed his drink, he looked towards the entrance of the hotel and seen the two women leaving. Karter threw a dub on the bar and left to go back up to his suite.

Knock Knock

Karter was so tipsy from the alcohol that he didn't realize the door was open.

"Come in!" He heard Cynthia say. My dumb ass didn't even see the door was open, thought Karter as he walked into the room. A smile instantly spread across his face when he seen Cynthia, butt ass naked in the bed, assumed in his favorite position, face down and ass up. Karter began undressing as he made his way to Cynthia. That night and the next 24 hours they stayed in the Penthouse Suite of the W. downtown, eating good, fucking good, and enjoying all of one another.

****

Elijah and Tasha had been at the hospital for two days. Tasha's pregnancy was being monitored by Dr.

Sinful Behavior

Watkins. Elijah and Tasha both were ready to go home. Tasha wasn't throwing up anymore and she was becoming irritated by being at the hospital. Elijah asked the nurse several times when would Tasha be discharged and she told him that the doctor would be the person to make that decision. Ten minutes later the doctor walked in.

"Am I glad to see you!" Said Tasha as soon as Dr. Watkins entered her room.

"How are you feeling, Misses Caine?" Dr. Watkins walked up to Tasha's bedside. The sound of his voice woke Elijah up out of his nap.

"I'm fine, but I'm ready to go home!" Tasha admitted.

"I understand Misses Caine, but there is an issue that we must discuss. Should we talk alone or are you fine with your companion being present?" Tasha looked at Elijah who was fully attentive, then she looked back at Dr. Watkins.

"Um, yeah! We can talk in front of my fiancé!" I really wish he would've asked me in privacy, thought Tasha as she grew nervous about what Dr. Watkins might say was wrong with her baby.

Michael "Oodoo" Smith

"Okay Misses Caine! We did blood work on you and we found a slight trace of pneumonia, plus you tested positive for HIV!" Dr. Watkins watched the life get drained from Tasha's face. Elijah felt like somebody hit him in the stomach with a sledgehammer.

"Nah! No fuckin way! I'm sorry doc, but you must've gotten her test mixed up or something with someone else's!" Elijah jumped up getting loud. Dr. Watkins almost became scared.

"Sir would you please calm down before I have to get security to escort you out!" Dr. Watkins warned Elijah, who started pacing the room.

"Baby please calm down!" Cried Tasha with tears overflowing from both of her eyes. Elijah went to Tasha's bedside and wrapped his arms around her neck.

"Don't worry baby! We are gonna get through this together!" He told Tasha.

"We are gonna have to keep you here for a few more days to get a blood sample from the baby to find out his status! Sir, it would be in your best interest to get tested also!" Dr. Watkins explained then he left out of the room. Fuck! I could be sick, thought Elijah and he let go of

Sinful Behavior

Tasha. He put his hands-on top of his head as he stepped back from her bed, then he walked to the window. He looked out into the sky and clouds. Then he dropped down to his knees and started crying.

"Lord please put your hands on me! Please bless me and my child to not be infected! Lord please!" Elijah begged. Tasha cried her heart out as she watched Elijah pray. She didn't know what to say to him. For the first time in years, she actually felt bad for a male species. She had been through so much, that she was really heartless towards a man. I can accept my lick because I've been living reckless up until I got with him, but I pray to God that him and my baby are not infected, thought Tasha as she watched Elijah pray, down on his hands and knees.

Tasha and Elijah didn't say anything to one another for what seemed like hours, but then the doctor came in and escorted Tasha to a room for the special procedure to get the baby's blood sample. Elijah took that time to take an AIDS test, then he left the hospital to go for a ride. So much was on his mind that he just wanted to be alone for a minute. So many what ifs and should nots were running through his brain that he was damn near going crazy. He decided to get him and Tasha something to eat before heading back to the hospital.

****

"Hey baby! How is your day going?" Karter asked Cynthia as he walked out of the gift store from picking up some roses and candies. Cynthia stepped inside an empty room to talk.

"After being boo'd up with my man for the past few days, this is hell!" Cynthia would've much rather been with Karter rather than at work.

"I know baby! I miss you too! What floor do they have you working?" Karter was missing Cynthia like crazy.

"They got me on the third floor and I'm glad! It's slow up here! I really don't feel like being bothered!"

"I miss you!" Karter hit up on the elevator

"I miss you too!"

"I'll call you later!"

"Okay baby!" Cynthia hung up then walked out of the room and bumped into a person walking down the hall.

Sinful Behavior

"Oh, excuse me! I'm so so _____!" Cynthia stopped talking when she realized who the person was that she bumped into.

"Hi Cynthia!" Elijah spoke softly.

"Hi Elijah!" Cynthia started walking away.

"Cynthia wait!" Elijah ran up to Cynthia, still holding his food and drinks in his hands.

"I don't have nothing to talk to you about! Now go kill yourself!" Karter seen and heard Cynthia tell Elijah as soon as the elevator door opened.

"You good baby?" Karter asked Cynthia while he mean mugged Elijah.

"Bayy! Yeah, I'm good! I don't know what he's doing up here!" Cynthia got on her tippy toes and kissed Karter. Elijah needed a friend, someone who he could confide in with his situation and the only two people that really knew him were standing in front of him.

"Tasha has HIV and the doctor is trying to make sure that the baby isn't infected!" Elijah couldn't hold it in any longer.

"You got what you were looking for!" Cynthia didn't care.

"Yeah and I got your baby! Are you hungry?" Karter pressed down on the elevator.

Ding

"Yeah baby!" Cynthia and Karter stepped on the elevator and left Elijah standing there looking stupid. Elijah was defeated as he watched Cynthia and Karter kiss while the elevator doors closed. He couldn't even get a conversation from his one-time best friend and his ex-wife. Elijah knew right then that it was time to start being a better father to his kids and a better friend to anyone that he communicated with.

****

The next few days were long and dry for Tasha and Elijah. They spoke the bare minimum to one another. I'm so sorry Elijah! I truly am, thought Tasha as a tear fell from her eye while she watched Elijah sleep in the chair next to her bed. Then she closed her eyes.

"Dear lord, I know I've been a devil on this earth, but I know that you're a forgiving God. I wanna thank you for everything that you've done for me. I came to you in

Sinful Behavior

prayer, begging you for one last request. Elijah and my baby are innocent bystanders of my bad decisions and wrongful actions, therefore my lord, I ask you to take my life and spare them of any harm or danger! In Jesus name I pray, Amen!"

That was deep, thought Elijah as he pretended to be asleep, but he was forced to open his eyes when the room door opened, and Dr. Watkins walked in.

"Good morning Misses Caine!"

"Good morning doc!" Tasha wiped her tears away.

"I have good news for you! Your child is not infected and since you're in your third trimester, I'm gonna induce your labor to bring your baby home! Is that fine with you?" Dr. Watkins asked Tasha.

"Yes! Cough! Cough!" Tasha nodded yes while she coughed.

"Okay! The nurses will be here in a few minutes to take you to the labor room!" Dr. Watkins turned to leave, but then he turned back around to Elijah.

"Oh yeah! Mr. Woods! Your test came back negative!" Dr. Watkins gave Elijah a thumbs up then left.

Elijah walked to Tasha's bedside. He could tell she was nervous.

"Everything is gonna be okay baby!" Elijah grabbed Tasha's hand and squeezed it.

"I know! God is gonna give me everything that I just asked him for!" Tasha smiled and tears traveled from her eyes. Her statement hit Elijah hard because he heard her prayer.

"Baby! You not gonna die! Elijah leaned down and kissed Tasha as tears fell from his eyes.

"This is the end Elijah! I love you!" Tasha assured Elijah. The door came open and two nurses walked in.

"Are you ready Misses Caine?" The younger of the two white nurses asked Tasha.

"Cugh, cugh, cugh, cugh! Yeah, cugh! I'm ready! Cugh!" Tasha placed her hand over her chest, which was hurting like hell every time she coughed.

"Okay! Can you get in the wheelchair for us?"

"Yeah!" Tasha rolled out of the bed and got into the wheelchair. Elijah followed as the nurses took Tasha to the labor room. He called Coretta Caine and told her what was going on while the nurses got Tasha situated in the bed.

"Here baby! It's mama!" Elijah handed Tasha his phone.

"I love you mama! I always have and I always will!" Tasha handed Elijah back the phone without even trying to listen to her mother. The nurses were about to get the doctor to come break Tasha's water, but her water broke on its own as soon as they got her hooked up to the IV's.

"I love you! Cugh, cugh!" She started coughing uncontrollably after she told Elijah that she loves him. Her chest was on fire.

"Call Dr. Watkins now!" One nurse told the other nurse, when Tasha's heart rate sped up tremendously.

"Baby are you okay?" Elijah leaned down and asked Tasha, but she couldn't respond to him because it was difficult for her to breathe.

"Ya'll go do something?" Elijah yelled at the nurses, he was scared and nervous.

"What's going on? Dr. Watkins asked as soon as he stepped into the room.

"We don't know! She won't stop coughing and her heart rate is abnormal!" The nurse explained while Dr. Watkins listened to Tasha's breathing with his stethoscope.

"Come on! We gotta get this baby out of her now!" Dr. Watkins didn't like what he heard in Tasha's chest.

"What's going on?" Elijah wanted to know.

"We've got to take her to have an emergency cesarean section!" Dr. Watkins explained while he helped the nurse transport Tasha's bed out of the room. Tasha started fading in and out of consciousness while they transported her. Elijah followed Tasha's bed. As soon as they turned the corner at the end of the hall, they were met by more nurses and another doctor as they wheeled Tasha into the delivery room.

"Put this on!" A nurse gave Elijah a mask and a scrub jacket to put on then he entered the room.

"Tasha baby!" Elijah tried to get Tasha's attention, but she was losing consciousness as the doctors cut her open to deliver the baby.

Sinful Behavior

"We're losing her!" Elijah heard one of the doctors say.

"Tasha baby, get up!" Cried Elijah.

"Whiiii!" Cried the baby.

"We lost her!"

"Try to revive her!"

"Step back, sir!" The doctor needed Elijah to move back so he could try to bring Tasha back, but there was no need, because she was gone.

"We're terribly sorry Mr. Woods, we couldn't save her. Here's your baby boy!" Dr. Watkins handed Elijah his newborn son.

Elijah smiled as his tears dropped down onto his son's face. He carried his son up to Tasha's dead body.

"We love you!" Elijah leaned down and kissed Tasha on her cold lips. This was Elijah's first time ever seeing prayer work so fast in such extreme measures. Everything Tasha prayed for came about in a matter of thirty minutes. God is nothing to play with, thought Elijah as he thought about Tasha's prayer.

"Elijah! Elijah! Elijah!" Cynthia shook Elijah out of his sleep.

"Huhh! Huhh!" Elijah jumped up out of his dream sweating like a mad man.

"Cynthia! Baby, it's you!" Elijah quickly realized that he was having a nightmare.

"Who else is it gonna be? Tasha or whoever name you were just screaming! You've been having one hell of a dream, haven't you? I've been trying to wake you up for the past hour. You kept scooting your butt up against me!" Cynthia wiped Elijah's face with a damp face cloth.

"Baby, I'm sorry if I've looked at another woman or thought about being with another woman. I love you baby! I'm gonna be the perfect husband from here on out!" Elijah pleaded.

"Baby where is all this coming from? You've been the perfect husband and father to our kids!" Cynthia was lost.

"Coretta's daughter, Tasha Caine tried to seduce me this morning at Sunday School!" Elijah admitted, Cynthia started laughing.

"What's funny baby?" Elijah was lost.

"Her and Karter just posted some pics on Facebook together claiming that they are in a relationship!" Cynthia explained.

"That's good news!" Better him than me, thought Elijah.

"Cynthia!"

"Yes baby!"

"Have you ever heard the saying "The Voodoo is in the DooDoo?" Elijah remember having that quote in his dream.

"No silly! What does that mean baby?"

"I don't ever want to know!"

Michael "Oodoo" Smith

More literary works available by author

AVAILABLE NOW

www.MichaelOoDooSmith.com

Sinful Behavior

More literary works available by author

AVAILABLE NOW

www.MichaelOoDooSmith.com

WHEN A GOOD GIRL GOES BAD 2: FROM ROCKS TO ROXYS

Michael "Oodoo" Smith

More literary works available by author

AVAILABLE NOW

www.MichaelOoDooSmith.com

Sinful Behavior

More literary works available by author

AVAILABLE NOW

THE G IN GAME 2

MICHAEL "OODOO" SMITH

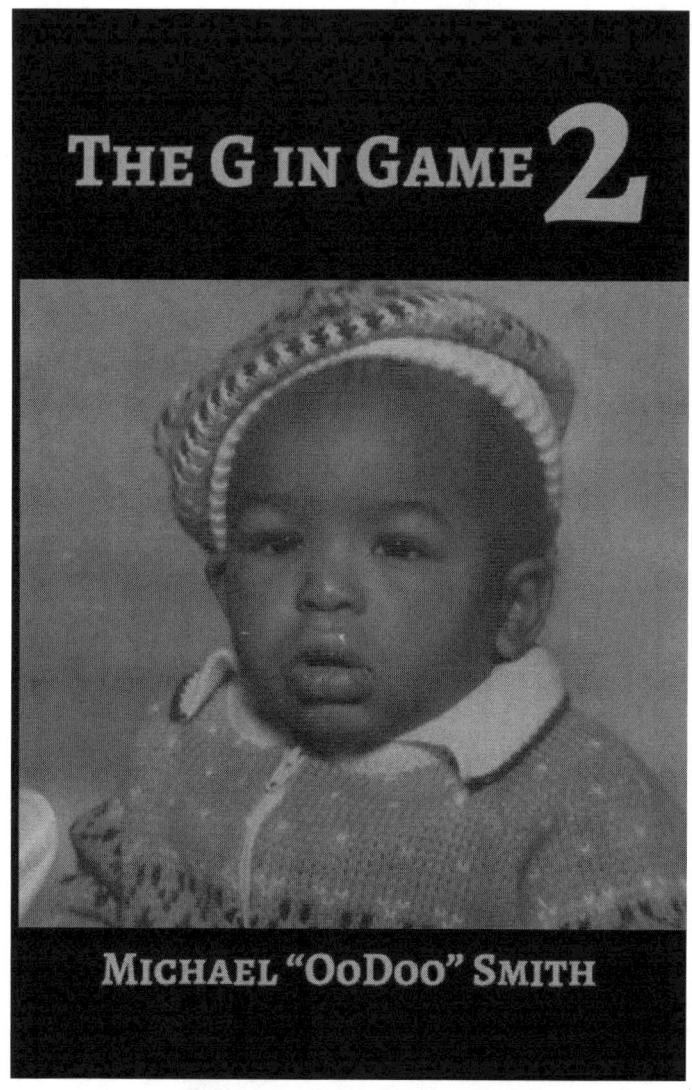

www.MichaelOoDooSmith.com

Made in the USA
Columbia, SC
18 June 2025